Pandora's Memories

BY JAMES YOUNG

Table of Contents

Dedication

To the men who flew the *Wildcat* in all its forms.

Prologue

The silence would have been total if not for the wind furiously blowing the tent's entry flap. All eyes were focused on the Marine major whom had just been singled out by Colonel Reginald Perry's question. The tall, patrician officer's blue eyes were narrowed as he focused on the shorter, stocky Marine. For his part, Adam met the colonel's icy gaze with an unwavering hazel glare of his own. It was clear, even in the dim light of the tent, that the Marine officer was not making any attempt to come to a position of attention.

"Sir, I'd prefer to defer to your judgment," Major Adam Haynes bit out, his tone making it clear just what he thought of Colonel Perry's deductive powers. "After all, while I have flown *several* aircraft, I have not flown the new models of the *Warhawk* or *Airacobra*."

Adam felt Lieutenant Colonel William Sloan, commander of the 1st Provisional Wing, stiffen beside him. He did not spare his commander a glance, knowing that the tall, sandy haired officer's face would be impassive no matter how pissed the man was at that particular instant.

I'm sorry, Sir, but if this asshole thinks he's bracing me... Adam thought.

"Major, you've been standing in the back of *my* briefing looking like you're sucking on a lemon throughout my talk.

4

Now I've watched you roll your eyes at my plan in clear view of myself and my flight commanders," Colonel Perry snapped. "I don't know how they do things in the Marine Corps, but in the *Army* we actually have some discipline."

"Colonel Perry, I don't think now…" Sloan began, his voice calm.

"*Lieutenant* Colonel Sloan, I don't give a damn what you think at this particular instant," Perry barked. "I'll talk to you later. But I'd like to hear what your pet mercenary has to say right now."

That tears it, Adam thought.

"Excuse me, gentlemen," he said, stepping past the Army officers who had the misfortune of standing in front of him in the packed medium tent. He strode up to the table, and for an instant fear flashed across Perry's eyes.

"You want to know what I think, *Sir*?" Adam asked. "I think you're a fucking idiot, and the men behind you are so green they piss grass."

There was a sharp intake of breath, but Adam pressed on despite Perry's face began to turn a sharp crimson.

"Their inexperience is the *only* reason you're getting away with proscribing your own personal Charge of the Light Brigade, and I'll be damned if *my* squadron will be staying around to get killed by a bunch of Germans. I hope *your* men enjoy dying in order to prove your bravery."

"*GET OUT!*" Perry roared, pointing at the tent entrance. Adam shook his head at the man as he turned towards the entrance. Quickly grabbing his trench coat, pile cap, and scarf, Adam stepped through the inner tent flap, every Army officer's eyes on him. Donning all of his outer garments as he heard Perry begin his briefing again, Adam shook his head and passed through the outer flap. A cold gust of wind slapped him in the face as he stalked towards the line of hangars roughly a hundred yards away.

Chapter 1: Reunion

Morton Ranch
Montana
1000 Local
23 December 1965

"I cannot believe one family owns this entire ranch," Natalia Cobb, nee Neuzora, flatly stated. "The Party would have divided this place into at least ten farms."

Major General Samuel "Sam" Michael Cobb, USMC, shook his head in bemused wonderment at his wife. Even after six years of living in the United States as a defector, two as Sam's spouse, Natalia retained a mild disgust for some aspects of American life. Dressed fashionably in a dark blue dress that matched her eyes, mid-length fur coat, and with her long blonde hair covered by a scarf, Natalia could have easily been a supermodel or movie star instead of the deadliest female ace in history.

Why have I always been attracted to the long-legged, deadly types? Sam asked himself, giving his wife and appreciative once over. It's not like…

"Perhaps you should pay attention to the road, Sam, rather than my legs," Nat said quietly. Sam whipped his head back to the front and immediately saw what had made his wife cautious. A large elk stood in the middle of the asphalt about a half mile ahead, coolly regarding the approaching automobile. Gently applying the brakes, Sam came to a stop well short of the animal. The cow looked to be in no hurry to move and, after a couple of minutes, Sam shut off the engine. As if that was the rest of the herd's cue, a line of other elk began to slowly meander behind the one in front of them.

Stupid animal, Sam thought, stretching his massive frame then running a hand through his close cropped hair.

"I am glad you were not so distracted when you faced the Germans," Natalia chided him, "or it is quite likely we would have never met."

Sam put his hand on her panty-hosed knee as he narrowed his sky blue eyes in a mock glare. Natalia fought down the urge to smirk, recognizing the predatory look he had as he leaned over the long bench seat.

"That would have been a crying shame," Sam said, then kissed her.

Minutes later, as his hand was traveling up her thigh, Natalia broke away from Sam with a slight gasp. Putting her hand on his chest, she pushed her husband firmly away.

"I think we should not be in, how do you say, *disarray* when we arrive to see Tabitha and her grandfather," Natalia said breathlessly. "Especially since I have no idea where I put my comb."

"Oh, I had no intentions of being in disarray, Ma'am," Sam drawled. "I was already thinking that if we just slipped into the guest cabin you'd have plenty of time to rearrange yourself." With that, his hand started sliding back up her leg.

"That may be, but wasn't Jacob expecting us soon?" Natalia asked, looking at him with a sternness that was not matched in her voice. "I'm sure he will be somewhat suspicious if we run off to the guest house rather than tell him we have returned from the theater," Nat replied, her cheeks coloring. A glint of sunlight on glass out of the corner of their eye made both of them turn around, heads nearly colliding in their haste.

"One would think that we were former aces or something," Sam chuckled. All too often, the glint of sunlight on a canopy had been the only warning that enemy aircraft were about, especially during Sam's campaign years.

"Yes, well, I see a car about five miles behind us," Natalia said. "I must say, this state is entirely too flat."

"Only in some parts," Sam replied, gesturing toward the mountains visible to their north.

"Although at least they have no daytime speed limit, unlike that torturous state in the middle of your country," Natalia observed. "What did you call it again? Oz?"

"No, honey, it was made famous by the *Wizard of Oz*. It's actually called Kansas."

"Well they should call it Hades in my opinion," Natalia replied with a shudder. "It's worse than Siberia."

"I don't know about all that," Sam said. "It at least has seasons."

"Siberia has seasons," Natalia said. "Pain, suffering, misery, and winter."

Sam looked agog at his wife, her face deadpan.

"Let's get up to Jacob's," he snorted, starting the car. Turning the blowers on max, he watched as the windshield's frog cleared.

Sam and Natalia's renewed progress was noted by the driver of the second car, even as his passengers both snored unawares. Pulling onto the long driveway that led up to the distant ranch house, Adam shook his head with a chuckle.

The eyes aren't as good as they used to be, but I can still see that back window is fogged over, Adam thought to himself. Sorry whomever you are if I just ruined your make out session.

"What's so funny, Dad?" Adam Jefferson Haynes III, or "Jeff", asked. Nineteen years old, the young man shared his father's fireplug build and hazel eyes yet combined these with his mother's red hair, pale skin, freckles and, in Adam's opinion, over developed sense of curiosity.

But, much as she did, he gets away with it because I love him, Adam thought.

"Oh, nothing," Adam replied as he reached over and shook his passenger to avoid giving Jeff time to press the issue.

Sure the boy's probably had a few make out sessions in a car himself, especially as the starting tight end for Idaho State, Adam thought. *Doesn't mean I need to give him any ideas.*

"Huh…what?" Josephine "Jo" Morton asked. "Oh wow, we made good time from Billings." She stretched, the movement proving as distracting to Adam as it had for the last seven months he'd known her. The wrinkles around her brown eyes and gray streaks in her shoulder length black hair were the only clues that the olive skinned woman was on the wrong side of forty. Much closer to five feet than six, Jo looked almost lost on her side of the Ford's bucket seat.

"You could say that" Adam replied with a smile.

"Why do I have the feeling that you didn't want to call my father or Tabitha before we left just so they wouldn't realize how good of time we made?" Josephine asked, arching her eyebrows.

"Tabitha worries too much, and your Dad still thinks aviators are insane," Adam replied. "Can you blame me for not wanting to listen to an hour solid of complaining?"

"Mom thought you were insane too," Jeff piped up from the backseat.

I don't know why he keeps mentioning his mother, Adam thought, but he's got about one more time…

"Your mother was a great woman," Jo said, attempting to defuse the situation. "I imagine Adam does think of her often.."

"How do you know what my mother was like? You never…" Jeff said, his tone strident.

"That's enough, Jeff," Adam snapped, meeting his son's eyes in the mirror. The young man looked like he was ready to say something else, but took one look at his father's face and thought better of it.

I can't turn you over my knee anymore, Adam thought. *But I will sure as hell make you walk the two miles to the ranch to teach you some manners.*

"I hope this isn't what I have to look forward to on your end," Adam muttered to Jo. Jeff turned from where he had been looking out the window, his eyebrows raised in curiosity.

"Oh, I'm sure Tabitha will be quite…happy to see you," Jo replied. Adam detected the slight pause and was about to start prying when there was an exclamation from the back seat.

"Holy shit! Elk!" Jeff said, then realized what he had said. "Sorry, Jo."

Adam fought down a smile.

Well that's one thing you did damn good on, Norah, Adam thought, sighing. I would have had the boy cussing like a sailor if you'd died earlier.

"Yes, the elk like it here since they know they're not going to end up dinner," Jo said. "Tabitha went crazy the first time she came up here. Some bull walked right up to

11

her bedroom window and looked in when she was getting some fresh air."

"Bet that's fun come spring," Adam said. "I'm not sure I'd want that many elk around with calves."

"Apparently the herd is pretty docile," Jo replied. It's almost like they don't want to ruin a good thing."

"Smart elk, knowing your father," Adam muttered, the remark getting him hit.

"Okay, who is Tabitha?" Jeff finally asked from the back seat. Adam, seeing an opportunity to get his son's goat, started to utter a sharp retort.

"Tabitha is my daughter," Jo said, giving Adam a look that stopped his sarcastic response in its tracks.

"Your daughter?" Jeff asked, his voice confused.

"Yes, my daughter," Jo replied with a smile.

"Jo was previously married," Adam said somberly.

"W-wha..? Who?" Jeff asked. "But I thought…"

"You thought that you already learned everything you needed to know about Jo from your classmates whom she taught in high school?"

"Why didn't you tell me?" Jeff queried, a twinge of hurt in his voice.

"Well, you were sort of busy being sullen that your Dad had started dating someone again that I didn't really get a chance," Adam chided. "Especially since most of your teammates seemed to know her from high school."

"You're not funny, Dad. You have no idea how badly I was teased over that."

"Oh, I have some idea," Adam replied. "I figured they would have mentioned Jo's daughter."

"Tabitha didn't go to public high school in Idaho," Jo said. "We used her Veterans and War Widows stipend to put her in private school."

Glad Congress decided to actually take care of people once the war was over, Adam thought. Then again, lots of widows from that madness and it helped that President Eisenhower served himself. Veterans and War Widows Act was the best thing to happen in 1955.

"Looks like someone was watching the road,"Adam said as they pulled up, seeing the front door starting to swing open. Putting the car into park, he hopped out and moved to open Jo's door. Finishing that task, he turned around to see the ranch's owner already standing just past the hood. Adam immediately came to attention and respectfully saluted the tall, thin figure.

"If you do that again, I will personally enjoy every moment I spend ripping limbs and appendages from your body," Admiral Jacob Thoreau Morton, recently retired Chief of Naval Operations, growled in utter seriousness as he returned the salute.

"Dad!" Jo said, her voice clearly mortified as she turned to her boyfriend. "Adam, I'm sorry, he's not usually this much of a curmudgeon." She gave the white haired man a look of sharp disapproval even as she walked over to give him a huge hug.

I can think of many captains, admirals, and Congressional members who would beg to differ, Adam thought.

"I don't need you going all Pavlovian on me, Mr. Haynes," Jacob said. "Part of the reason I came out here to Montana was to get away from that crap."

"Well, Sir, are you…"

"Stow it!" Jacob barked. With wizened features to go with the full head of snow white hair, Jacob definitely resembled his nickname "The Stork". Bestowed upon him by his classmates, the moniker had become public knowledge when Franklin Roosevelt had hung the Medal of Honor around his neck. While lacking the same masculine air as "Bull" Halsey, the nation had grown fond of the sobriquet due to repeated exposure.

"Dad!" If anything, Jo's voice sounded even more anguished than before as she reacted to Jacob's snapped command.

"Granddaddy, what have you done now?"

Turning, Adam saw a younger, taller version of Jo push open the door.

Okay, she must get her height from her father, Adam thought in disbelief, as the young woman was at eye level with Jacob despite wearing flats. Dressed in a clingy, rainbow-striped top and a skirt that was far shorter than anything Adam would have let an immediate female family member wear, Tabitha pulled on the jacket she left the house with and shivered slightly.

If I was twenty…well, okay, twenty-five years younger, she'd definitely catch my eye, Adam thought as he watched the tall woman embrace her mother with a happy squeal. Her raven hair hung loosely past her shoulders, blowing in the Montana wind.

"Close your mouth boy, you'll draw flies," Jacob barked, looking past Adam. Adam turned to see his son blushing and following the older man's advice, suddenly turning to pop the trunk.

Wait, I forgot I brought my younger alter ego, Adam thought wryly. Better watch him or else Admiral Morton will be feeding him his own bal…

"Granddad!" Tabitha said, her voice almost an echo of her mother's earlier indignation.

"Well, if you'd wear a decent amount of clothing rather than what's fashionable, I wouldn't have to be embarrassing you now would I?"

"Jacob, what has you all in a bother?" called a voice from inside, the Southern drawl strongly familiar to Adam's ears. "You'd think that you saw a rattlesnake or…"

Sam stopped dead as he stepped out and saw Adam standing in the front yard. Both men let out a simultaneous whoop and ran towards each other, embracing like long lost brothers. Adam felt his ribs creak as Cobb squeezed and lifted him off the ground.

Dumb ox always didn't know his own strength, Adam thought.

"Holy crap, what are you doing here?!" Sam exclaimed, letting Adam go.

"I could ask you the same question!" Adam replied excitedly. Turning, he saw Jo was standing there with an impish smile on her face.

"Did you know about this?!" Adam asked, a broad grin on his face.

"Perhaps," Jo replied coquettishly. Adam felt his heart swelling with emotion.

I haven't seen Sam Cobb in almost two years, he thought. *Yet you set this up to surprise me? I don't care who's watching*. With that, Adam swiftly swept Jo back and kissed her, eliciting Tabitha and Jeff's mutual, vocal disgust.

"I love you," Adam said when they broke. Jo, blushing, nodded her eyes slightly moist.

"You haven't heard why you're both here yet," she said as Adam let her stand back up.

"Why is that?" Sam asked, his voice suddenly wary. "I just thought we were here to have some time away from civilization."

"Uh, actually not quite," Jo said, looking over at Tabitha.

"Uncle Sam, Mr. Haynes, I need a favor," Tabitha said.

Adam looked at Sam, raising an eyebrow. Cobb shrugged, shaking his head to indicate he had no idea either.

"Why do I get the feeling that she only calls you Uncle Sam when she wants something?" Adam asked.

"Well, that and when she's in trouble," Sam said, giving Tabitha a look.

"Uh, not to intrude, but could someone explain to me why she's calling you Uncle Sam?" Jeff asked. "Because the last time I checked, Uncle Sam's the guy on the poster."

"Remember how I said that Jo had been married before?" Adam asked.

"Yeah," Jeff said, and then suddenly started to get cognition. "Wait..."

"I'm her brother-in-law," Sam said quietly in confirmation, seeing the look on the younger boy's face. "Jo was married to my brother Eric."

Jeff looked over at Jo, who for her part was staring off over the Montana plains. Adam, realizing why, moved over and put his arm around her.

"I'm okay," she said softly, the slight trembling of her shoulders indicating that she was a liar. Looking back, Adam could see a stricken look on Jeff's face.

"Son, why don't you finish getting the stuff out of the trunk and taking it to the guest house?" Adam asked. "Jo and I are going to take a walk."

Jeff looked around, his face getting more and more shocked as Adam and Jo started to stride off. Adam watched as he turned to Sam and Jacob, both of whom were similarly somber.

"I'm sorry," Jeff said quietly.

"Don't worry about it, son, you didn't do anything wrong," Jacob said. "Sam, why don't we go inside and let the young people work off some of that youthful exuberance?"

"Sounds good," Sam replied. "I think we're going to need some coffee."

"Funny you should mention that," Jacob replied as the door closed behind them.

"Okay, could someone explain to me what made the old folks go all melancholy?" Jeff asked after the door closed.

"Long story," Tabitha replied. "I can tell you while we're getting your bags out."

"Okay," Jeff said, turning to the trunk. He grabbed his Dad's footlocker and started pulling.

"Hey, let me help you out with that."

Jeff stopped as Tabitha grabbed the other handle. Looking over at the attractive young woman, Jeff suddenly found himself at a loss for words. Fortunately for him, his companion had no such problem.

"Well, as you can guess, I'm Tabitha," she grunted as the two of them lifted the box out and onto the ground. Letting go of her handle, Tabitha extended her hand. Jeff took it, making a conscious effort to avoid staring at her chest.

She obviously takes care of herself, Jeff thought, surprised at the firmness of Tabitha's grip.

"I'm Jeff. Well, actually I'm Adam too, but everyone calls me Jeff," he stammered, then stopped.

*Smooth, however, is **not** my middle name*, he thought, tongue tied.

"Well Jeff who is actually Adam," Tabitha teased, "as you can tell just about everyone here knows everyone else. Uncle Sam and your Dad used to fly together in the war."

"When Dad was in Russia or Okinawa?" Jeff asked. The last caused a shadow to fall over Tabitha's face.

"Both, actually, but Uncle Sam worked for him in Russia."

"Oh, okay. You'll have to excuse me, but I don't know all that much about when Dad was in the war," Jeff said. "He doesn't like talking about it to anyone."

"I know," Tabitha replied, drawing a look of surprise from Jeff. "I mean, I know about the last part," Tabitha stammered with a grimace.

"Why is that?"

"Because I need him and Uncle Sam to tell me about one of their missions for a scholarship paper," Tabitha replied.

"Huh?"

"I'm getting my Masters at Berkeley," Tabitha said, causing Jeff to look at her in shock.

"You don't…"

"Look that old?" Tabitha asked, her voice self-conscious. "It's because I'm not. I skipped three grades growing up and finished up college a year early."

"What?"

"Yeah, I'm what some people call a nerd," Tabitha said quietly. Jeff gave her an up and down look, then mentally slapped himself. Fortunately, Tabitha took it the wrong way.

"You know, you don't have to look at me like I'm some freak from the movies," she snapped. Jeff held up his hands defensively.

"I was just thinking that you didn't look like any nerd I'd ever seen," Jeff said, then caught himself. "I meant, you didn't look like a freak at all. No, wait, I didn't…"

Tabitha giggled at him as he blushed.

"I understand what you meant, and thank you," she said, smiling. "Now, back to what I was trying to explain, the Naval Institute is having a Veteran's Child Scholarship Contest, open to anyone who is the child of a living or deceased veteran of World War Two, the German Revolution, or the Balkans' War of '64."

Jeff looked over to where Adam and Jo were walking around the ranch's buildings.

"Now why wasn't I told about this?" Jeff mused.

"Because your Dad doesn't like to think about the war, probably," Tabitha said. "I know Uncle Nick flat out refuses to discuss it. But that could be because he was always taking care of grandma."

"Uncle Nick? Your Mom has a brother?" Jeff asked, his tone clearly indicating he was starting to wonder what else no one had told him.

"No, actually he's on my Dad's side," Tabitha replied wistfully. "There were once Cobbs aplenty, until the Krauts decided five were too many. Then the Japs took one too, son-in-law meant Hirohito had two, and the Lord said that's hurt aplenty."

Jeff looked at Tabitha in shock at her nursery rhyme.

"My Aunt Patricia made that ditty up a couple years after the war ended," Tabitha said. "Tends to end the discussion when people get nosy about Uncle David or my father."

She held up her hands as Jeff opened his mouth to start an apology.

"I'm the one telling you the family story," she said with a chuckle. Even Jeff, as thickheaded as he was, could sense the lack of mirth behind it. Tabitha wrapped her arms around herself, and suddenly Jeff didn't think it was because she was cold.

"My father's name was Eric Cobb," she said softly. "He was a fighter-bomber pilot with the Fifth Fleet back when we invaded Japan."

Jeff mentally winced, suddenly knowing where this was going.

"He was shot down on September 2, 1945. Uncle Sam, your father, and Dad were all flying on the same mission but with different squadrons," Tabitha continued. "The reason they were so happy to see one another is that they've only seen each other a couple of times since that day."

"My God," Jeff said, suddenly having the urge to reach out and comfort Tabitha. Putting impulse into action, he started to step towards her when she held up her hand.

"I appreciate you wanting to comfort me, but my grandfather's watching from the kitchen window," Tabitha said quietly. "He's sort of old-fashioned about the whole touching thing."

"Oh," Jeff said.

"Mom says it's because of something that happened when she was a teenager," Tabitha said quietly.

"I'm so sorry," Jeff said.

"Why? You didn't kill my father," Tabitha replied bitterly.

"I'm sorry you didn't grow up with a parent," Jeff replied somberly. "I know a little bit about that."

Tabitha turned to look at him, a sardonic smile on her face.

"Well, that means you can officially stay at the homestead," she said lightly, her eyes wet. "You have to lose someone you love in order to fit in here."

Jeff looked over at where his father and Jo were standing by a tree. The couple embraced, Adam looking over Jo's head at Jeff and Tabitha.

"Dad's going to help you," Jeff said, smiling.

"How do you know?" Tabitha asked, perplexed.

"He's got the same look on his face he did when Martin Caidin came by the house."

"Who's Martin Caidin?"

"Only the best aviation author of the last twenty years," Jeff said. "And one of three people to get Dad to talk about his past."

"Only three?" Tabitha asked, suddenly crestfallen.

"Dad's been around a bit," Jeff replied grimly. "People don't like revisiting events that put blood on their hands, especially when there's not enough soap in the world to wash it off."

"That's morbid," Tabitha said, causing Jeff to look at her.

Wait, weren't you just giving me a little ditty about how to remember who is dead in the family?

"Just wait until Dad starts talking," Jeff said. "Let's get this luggage inside before you get pneumonia, or I get the feeling your grandfather will beat my behind."

"You're scared of my grandfather?" Tabitha asked, incredulous. "You're twice his size!"

"Old age and treachery trumps youth and exuberance, and anyone my Dad respects enough to salute probably has an extra large helping of orneriness in them," Jeff replied simply. "esides, you're starting to look like a popsicle."

Tabitha gave a sound of shock and hit Jeff on the arm. To his surprise, it actually hurt.

Seems like being a strong woman runs in the Morton family, he thought. *Or is it the Cobb side?*

"Come on, at this rate we're not going to have time to set up the map."

"What map?" Jeff asked, perplexed. "What do you mean, 'we?'"

Tabitha turned to look at him, raising an eyebrow.

"You want to be put to work by me, or by my grandfather?" she asked archly.

"Grab the handle," Jeff said, picking up his end of the footlocker without hesitation.

Chapter 2: Preparations

Morton Ranch
1300 Local
23 December 1965

"Thanks Adm…Mister Morton, for having us out here," Adam said, having to fight not to use Jacob's wartime rank.

"You're welcome, Mr. Haynes," Jacob replied, his tone mocking Adam's formality.

Sam chuckled as he added cream to his own coffee.

"You have a problem, Sam?" Jacob asked archly.

"You have no idea how amusing it is to see Adam like this," Sam said. "This was a man who terrorized VMF-21 when he took it over, and here he is, being all meek and polite."

"You can credit the women I've had in my life," Adam said. "They've taught me manners, unlike you."

"I am a Russian, not a miracle worker," Nat said from the kitchen counter where Jo and she stood making sandwiches. "I could sooner cause peace on earth than I could teach Sam etiquette."

"Ouch!" Sam said. "My mother would tell you I have perfectly good manners, thank you very much."

"To which I would reply, 'Only in the bedroom,'" Nat snapped back in Russian. Sam looked at her, utterly mortified as both Jo and Adam burst into laughter.

"Honey, they both speak Russian!" he said. "Jo teaches Russian for God's sake."

Natalia blushed a brilliant shade of red as Jacob turned to look at Sam.

"There's no need to take the Lord's name in vain," Jacob said solemnly. "Although I'm sure, judging from Jo's face, that mild blasphemy pales to whatever was said."

"This from a man who once said, 'I don't want a Goddamned Jap alive when we're done'?" Sam asked. "I'm sorry, when did you get religion again, Jacob?"

Jacob gave Sam a hard look.

"Fine, I may have said some things in the heat of battle that I shouldn't have," Jacob admitted. "I just don't want you speaking that way around my granddaughter when she's asking you for your help."

"Where is Tabitha, anyway?" Sam asked.

"She's busy getting the dining room arranged how she likes it," Jacob said. He continued with clear disdain, "It appears she's got a helper."

Jo and Adam looked at one another, then back at Jacob.

"What has Jeff done?" Adam asked slowly.

"Oh, he hasn't done anything, just probably thought about doing several things that better not happen on this homestead."

"Jeff's a good boy," Adam replied defensively.

"Yeah, I've heard that before," Jacob replied, a look passing between him and his daughter. Adam looked at Jo with a raised eyebrow.

"It would take far too much time to explain," Jo said.

"Not really," Sam volunteered, earning him a huge glare from his former sister-in-law.

"That's all right, you can tell me when you're ready," Adam replied.

The door to the dining room opened, Tabitha poking her head out.

"Speaking of the devil," Sam said, causing his niece to look at him quizzically. Adam saw that the young woman had changed clothes, wearing a baggy sweatshirt and jeans with her black hair pinned up in a ponytail. A clear pair of reading glasses were perched atop her bangs, making her look like a stereotypical young librarian.

"Ladies and gentlemen, if you could join me?"

"Why of course, my little bookworm," Jo said with mock gravitas.

"Mom," Tabitha said, her voice carrying a child's exasperation, "it's hard for others to be serious if you're not."

Jo was clearly taken aback.

"What, has being a graduate student suddenly made you all prim and proper? I thought Berkeley was all peace, love, and happiness."

"Not in the History Department. There it's rum, sodomy, and the lash," Tabitha said, completely straight-faced. The five adults all looked at her in shock, Jacob actually having to catch his coffee mug. Unable to keep up her pretenses at her grandfather's near fumble, Tabitha started giggling.

"Sorry, just got through taking Maritime Strategy with Dr. Phelps," she said. "He's a big fan of the Royal Navy."

Adam laughed, suddenly drawing the connection. The other four adults turned to look at him, and he suddenly stopped, embarrassed.

"I know you're getting your Masters in history, but what part again? I only ask because Jeff's a history major too," Adam said quickly, changing the subject.

"My Masters is in American Grand Strategy, with an emphasis on the 20th Century," Tabitha replied.

"The century's barely half over," Adam remarked dryly. "Although I guess there's been enough killing to fill a course load."

"And with that cheery thought, let's get to work," Sam said, pushing back from the table. Jo grabbed Adam as he was about to start through the door.

"You want to explain the sodomy comment?" she whispered in his ear.

"Churchill," Adam said. "Commenting on Royal Navy tradition."

"Ah," Jo said, still confused. "I was just starting to wonder what kind of company you kept before I knew you."

"I flew with Sam...do you really need to ask?"

"Point,"Jo replied with a slight laugh.

Walking into the dining room, it was easy to see why Jacob usually took his meals in the kitchen. The cavernous space's long edge was at least twenty-five feet long, with its short edge about half of that. The room was dominated by a large, square table that looked big enough to seat six around each side when it wasn't in its current condition, i.e. covered by a large aviator's map and several books. Jeff was busy placing small scale aircraft on the surface, a look of concentration on his face as he kept referring to a heavy book in his hand. Looking at the front, Adam could see that the tome was actually in Russian, the title in scarlet, block Cyrillic letters.

"Okay Uncle Sam, if you and Mr. Haynes could sit about where Jeff is now standing, I'd greatly appreciate it," Tabitha said.

Adam and Sam gave each other a bemused look, then took the directed chairs.

"Aunt Nat, if you could sit on the north side of the map once you guys are done? Thanks."

"Where do you want me?" Jeff asked. Tabitha gave him a speculative look, then decided.

"Well, you can be the Germans, so I need you to sit opposite of Uncle Sam and Adam."

"Jeff, did you mention to Tabitha that you speak fluent German as well as Russian?" Adam asked, seeing a couple of texts sitting on the "west" side of the map. Tabitha looked up sharply at this statement, then gave Jeff a hard look.

"Uh, no, but thanks Dad," Jeff said, giving Tabitha a sheepish shrug.

"Anytime, boy, anytime," Adam replied.

I'm not saying he's a knucklehead, but he's definitely in for a fun time if their chemistry keeps cooking, Adam thought, looking at Jeff. While no one would confuse his son for a village idiot, odds were they wouldn't think he'd won a Nobel Prize either.

"You know, Tabitha, this looks like a lot of work," Jo said. "What exactly is it?"

"I've figured out the location of all Allied and German units down to the individual squadrons," Tabitha replied. The statement led to an appreciative whistle from her grandfather as he sat in the corner and began fiddling with a pipe.

"If you've gotten that much work done on this, I don't know what you need us for?" Sam said, his voice indicating his own impression.

"Well, namely because the primary Russian sources are contradictory and the Germans prefer not to mention the 23 December raid in their wartime histories."

"People tend to be hesitant to talk about a one-sided a…I mean, butt-whuppin' when they're on the wrong side," Adam said, mindful of the ladies present. Jeff stifled a laugh at his father's discomfiture.

"Oh no, Mr. Haynes, don't censor yourself on my account," Tabitha said. "I need you to say the first thing that comes to mind when you're talking."

"Oh no, I don't think you want Adam to revert back to his pre-Norah days," Sam said, then stopped as he realized it was impolite to talk about someone's previous spouse.

"You make it sound like Dad used to curse quite a bit," Jeff said.

"Trust me, if you knew your Dad when he was our commander, you'd think there wasn't enough soap in the world to clean his mouth."

"I was not that profane," Adam said defensively.

"Liars go to Hell," Sam drawled, rolling his eyes. "You tell that big of a fib again you'll have your own train."

"Thanks, Sam," Adam said incredulously.

"No problem, Buccaneer Lead," Sam replied with a grin.

"Why didn't you try to use their battle reports, Tabitha?" Jacob asked from the corner as he lit his pipe. Sam and Adam looked at one another, then burst into laughter. No one listening actually mistook the sound as containing any joy.

"We sort of didn't write many action reports," Adam replied grimly. "That would've required us to not be flying about four sorties a day."

"Your Army counterpart, thankfully, found time to jot down what happened during the battle," Tabitha replied.

"What?!" Sam asked, his voice rising.

"Which one?" Adam snapped simultaneously.

"Major Mark Price," Tabitha said defensively, crossing her arms and leaning back from the two men's vehemence.

Adam and Sam shared a haunted look.

"How about you let us hear what he said, then we'll explain why he had so much time," Sam replied grimly.

"All right then, let's get started," Tabitha said, giving her uncle a strange look. Reaching under the table, she pulled out a large case. Opening it, she revealed a reel-to-reel tape recorder, complete with microphone.

"Everyone ready?" she asked. "Okay, good, here we go." Starting the device, she brought the microphone up to her mouth as she approached the table.

"Today's date is December twenty-third, 1965. I am here with Brigadier General, retired, Adam J. Haynes, and Major General Samuel M. Cobb, both United States Marine Corps. Other individuals present will be included in the notes for the written transcript."

Pausing, Tabitha looked at the map to collect her thoughts.

"Gentlemen, why don't you tell me what you thought of the situation in December 1943," Tabitha said.

Adam looked at Sam, who shrugged. He motioned for Tabitha to pause the tape.

"What are you looking for, exactly?" Adam asked. "I mean, I'm sure you're not expected to talk about Hitler or King George VI's deaths, the Second Battle of Britain, the problem with English succession, or Stalin's stroke, are you?" he asked.

"Well, no," Tabitha allowed. "But maybe a little bit about how you ended up in the Soviet Union?"

"Okay," Adam said, then grabbed his water. Taking a big drink, he pursed his lips then nodded for Tabitha to continue.

"We got our orders to head to the Soviet Union in mid-October of '43," he stated evenly. "When they'd attacked the Germans, the Soviets had gotten over half their air force destroyed. The German counteroffensive took care of most of the rest. With the *Luftwaffe* wreaking havoc, the Triumvirate asked President Roosevelt for help."

"Did you know any of this when you got your orders?" Tabitha asked.

"No," Adam replied. "We were supposed to be transitioning to *Corsairs* and heading out to Hawaii. Then came word that we would instead be drawing FM-2s."

"Could you explain that in a couple of sentences?" Tabitha asked. "I'm not great with planes."

"The *Corsair* was probably the best fighter the Marines flew in the war," Adam replied simply. "The FM-2 was a slightly improved variant of the fighter we started the war with, the F4F *Wildcat*. Which is to say we went from getting told we were getting a brand new sports car to just a new engine in our old clunker."

"I'm not sure I'd say the *Wildcat* was a clunker," Sam interjected. "It was tough, the guns packed a punch, and it was more maneuverable than anything we faced in those first six months."

"Which is like saying a woman's not hideous from the neck down," Adam responded.

"Adam!" Jo said in horror, causing Tabitha to give an exasperated sigh as she rewound the tape.

"If you two could keep your lovers' quarrels off my tape?" Tabitha muttered loudly.

"Yes bookworm," Jo said.

"What Adam's not telling you is that, having fought in Spain and during the Second Battle of Britain, he knew how to capitalize on the *Wildcat*'s strengths and mitigate its weaknesses," Sam stated once Tabitha restarted the tape.

Adam shrugged.

"It was my job to keep you guys from getting killed," he said grimly.

"Some people certainly didn't enjoy the way you did that," Sam declared with a smile.

"How so?" Tabitha asked.

"Let's just say Adam had a way with our sister services," Sam replied. As he recounted the story of Colonel Perry's briefing, Adam reached over and grabbed a sandwich. Jo rubbed his back as he did so, then leaned in close to his ear.

"Thank you," she whispered simply.

"You can thank me later," Adam growled lowly.

"Oh, I plan to," Jo replied mischievously, causing Adam to choke on the bite of sandwich. Tabitha pushed pause on the tape again.

"Mother!"

"What? It's not my fault the man can't chew his food."

Adam squeezed her knee under the table at that comment.

"Sorry, I was distracted," Adam said, once his throat was clear. "Please continue."

I'm as nervous as a cat in a room full of rocking chairs, Adam thought. *But if there's ever a group I can get through this with, these folks would be it.*

"So why did the Germans attack the Moscow rail center with their older He-111s and Ju-88s rather than their He-

177s?" Tabitha asked, referring to the *Luftwaffe*'s heavy bomber.

"For one, they were using those to attack the Soviet factories in the Urals," Adam said. "Of course, they didn't realize they were mainly striking at decoys, which was why the Red Air Force was only putting up token resistance. They just thought they'd killed enough Russian pilots that the Soviets weren't able to put up enough fighters."

"They weren't that far off," Sam interrupted. "If it hadn't been for the Germans outrunning their logistics and the autumn rain, the Germans probably would have gotten to Moscow before we did."

"Well, that and the decision to go to Leningrad," Adam allowed. "I'm thinking getting mauled up north didn't help their army any."

"Should've laid siege to the place," Jacob growled. "Couldn't have held out for more than a few months without food."

"You would be surprised what Russian can endure," Natalia said grimly. "I think it was more the three weeks of sacking the city that caused the delay. My mother's family was from there—the stories are truly horrible. Starving to death would have been a blessing."

"My apologies," Jacob replied sheepishly.

"You weren't the person raping and pillaging," Natalia said simply. "But I do not think the young scholar needs to hear about German soldiers."

While the Red Army had a tendency to stick its head in nooses then dare the Germans to kick the chair, Adam thought, *no one can dispute they fought like lions. Too bad they didn't have gas masks or they might have held.*

"So why didn't the Germans attack Moscow with nerve gas like they did London?" Tabitha asked.

Adam and Sam shared a look.

"Pause the tape," Sam said after a moment, his voice stern. Tabitha did so.

"The Germans couldn't keep up their nerve gas production with what they were doing in those camps," Sam growled, his voice husky. "They used up all their military reserves at Leningrad, and Heydrich was more interested in his SS killing Jews than helping the *Wehrmacht* kill Russians."

Tabitha paled.

"You know that's never been put down anywhere, Uncle Sam?" she replied.

"It has," Jacob fumed from the corner. "Just not anywhere you would have had access to it."

"It's getting declassified next month," Sam replied to the former admiral's rebuke. "Guess President Eisenhower decided he's tired of people asking why we didn't rush to the Germans' aid quicker back in '52."

"It was mentioned in some of our briefings," Natalia stated. "I just thought it was propaganda."

Tabitha chewed on her lip.

"You know, I'd get the paper for sure if I included something that new," she said quietly.

"You'd also get your uncle tossed in jail," Adam replied, drawing a nod of agreement from Jacob. "Just consider it a case of you know something other people don't."

"I should get Mom to help me out more often," Tabitha observed.

"Must be nice," Jeff interjected archly, causing Adam to set his coffee down more heavily than normal.

"If you have a problem with something, we can talk later," the elder Haynes snapped. "Family business."

Jeff closed his mouth with an annoyed sigh as Jo shifted beside Adam.

Yes this is probably as close to family as one can get without marriage, Adam thought. *Still not airing our dirty laundry here.*

Tabitha started her tape again with a flair, clearly becoming annoyed at all the interruptions.

"What I was thinking now is that we would go around the table in chronological order, starting with you, Mr. Haynes and Uncle Sam, then letting Jeff read from *Commonwealth Leader* for the Commonwealth side…"

"You know, if you had given me some advance warning I probably could've got Wing Commander O'Rourke out here," Adam said.

"Well, we've got his book," Tabitha said. "Mom wasn't sure you'd come."

Adam shrugged, giving Jo an apologetic look.

"She's probably right. Sorry I interrupted, you were saying?"

"Jeff can also read Stephen Haas's *Bomber Pilot for the Reich* since he's fluent," Tabitha said, giving Adam's son a hard look, "while Aunt Nat reads from *Women for the Rodina!*"

"So how will we know to tell you what we were doing?" Sam asked.

"I've taped little index cards with the times on each passage, so if you or Mr. Haynes could interrupt whenever we reach a time that you were doing something, I'd greatly appreciate it."

"Gee, it's only been twenty-five years sweetie…half the time I can't even remember what I had for dinner last night, much less the exact time things happened," Sam said, his voice concerned.

"I've got a pretty good idea when things happened," Adam said grimly. "There are some days in your life you don't forget, even if you've had hundreds like them."

"Thanks Mr. Haynes," Tabitha said, genuinely grateful as she saw the haunted look that crossed his face. "If we need stop at any time..."

"Don't worry, I'm not going to start screaming incoherently over your interview," Adam said. "I save that for when I'm sleeping."

Both Jeff and Jo shifted uncomfortably, each remembering instances of the nightmares Adam was referring to. Adam gestured for Tabitha to start the tape recorder again.

"It was around 1100 and cold as hell when we got ready to take off."

Chapter 3: Remembrances

Moscow #6 North
1105 Local
23 December 1943

Adam looked at his flight commanders one last time, meeting each man's eyes in turn.

"Remember, no more than two passes, dammit!" he barked. "I don't care what that West Point idiot says on the other side of the strip, as soon as we hit the bombers there will be German fighters everywhere. If you want to be alive tonight, don't be there when they arrive."

The officers all nodded, their faces showing the whole gamut of emotions from fear to excited anticipation. Adam looked at Captain Bowles, his Green Flight Leader, and had to keep a look of utter satisfaction from crossing his face. Scion of a naval family, Bowles had been a thorn in Adam's side since he had taken over VMF-21, the "Flying Buccaneers."

Guess your Daddy's friends can't save you now, you asshole, Adam thought triumphantly without a shred of regret. *Either you're going to get it together, or you're going to get a chop that string pulling can't save you from.* As he watched, the pallid captain swallowed, beads of sweat on his face despite the bitter cold.

I hope your wingman's as smart as I think, Adam thought. *Don't want to lose both of you because you're an idiot.*

Adam turned and regarded Sam Cobb next. The tall Southerner had the look of someone who expected to go upstairs and kill lots and lots of Germans without working too hard at it.

Cobb has the same look Don Blakeslee used to get during Second Britain, Adam thought. I'd have that look too if I flew better than Death himself.

There were several shotgun blasts a few meters away, the sound causing Bowles to jump as VMF-15 started their engines. Equipped with older F4F *Wildcats*, the "Black Knights" mounts used the shells to initiate the ignition process. The short, stubby fighters looked identical to the FM-2s flown by Adam's squadron, except their wings had six rather than four .50-caliber machine guns. He watched as the first of the Black Knights navy blue aircraft began to waddle towards the end of the runway.

Thing looks like an overweight duck on the ground, Adam thought bitterly. *Glad we've got the ones with more powerful engines.* Looking at his watch, he shook himself out of the melancholy frame of mind. No use fretting, one goes to war with the aircraft at hand. Which is why we're going to hit and run.

"I will have 1115 hours on my mark," Adam said. Making sure all three flight leaders had their hands on their watches, he continued. "Mark! Good luck, gentlemen. Give the final briefing to your flights, takeoff will be in ten minutes. Dismissed." Returning the three salutes, Adam turned to head for his own *Wildcat* and nearly ran straight into Lieutenant Colonel Sloan.

"Bowles looks a little peaked," Sloan said, an uncharacteristic frown on his face. "He doesn't have the trots, does he?"

"No Sir, he's just got a case of the 'scared shitless,'" Adam said flatly. "He'll either get over it or we'll be boxing up his stuff tonight."

Sloan gave Adam a hard look, well aware of the major's hatred of Bowles.

"You know, you'd be a lot better liked by your peers and subordinates if you didn't try to be such a hard ass all the time," the lieutenant colonel observed, shaking his head. "Colonel Perry wanted to place you under arrest for calling him an idiot in front of his flight commanders last night."

Adam looked askance at his commander, one eyebrow raised. Colonel Perry nominally outranked the Marine. If Sloan had decided that situation gave the Army officer authority over the entire American Air Expeditionary Force, things were about to get interesting.

Sloan's looking at me like I should be apologizing, Adam thought. After a few moments, during which Sloan realized Jesus Christ would be walking across the runway before Adam expressed any remorse, the exasperated lieutenant colonel continued.

"I told him that I would not have my squadron leaders' opinions second-guessed, nor would I allow him to dictate the doctrine that we would fight by," Sloan continued, his voice clipped. "Colonel Perry then attempted to pull rank, at which point I reminded him we were not under his command and he could kiss my ass."

Adam looked at his commander with newfound respect. Until that moment, he had believed Sloan was a careerist, someone who had simply gotten promotions by staying in the Corps long enough. Now, he saw that he had underestimated the man's capabilities as a leader in the short time they'd been together.

"Thank you, Sir," Adam said sincerely. Sloan gave a half-smile.

"First human thing I've heard you say or do since we got shuffled together. Don't worry, I won't tell your squadron that you've actually got a heart," the superior officer said with a wink. Then his face grew serious as they walked towards Adam's fighter. "However, Perry intends to get our command relationship 'clarified' as soon as he gets back."

"Sir, he's not coming back," Adam said simply. Sloan nearly stumbled as he turned to look at him.

"Please tell me you're not contemplating murder, Major Haynes," he said, darkly. Adam looked at him deadpan, then was not able to contain his laughter.

"I see nothing funny about this," Sloan snapped. Adam managed to get control of his laughter, realizing the tension was making him loopy.

"Sir, I'd desert and bike over to the Commonwealth Wing before gunning down a friendly pilot," Adam managed to say without smiling. "No matter whether that son of a bitch deserves it or not, I still have to sleep at night."

"So the heartless former mercenary does have some scruples after all. Although I fail to see what good would going over to the Commonwealth Wing does you." Sloan stated, narrowing his eyes. "I thought they had more pilots than planes."

"Wing Commander O'Rourke and I go back a ways," Adam stated with a grin. "We don't tell many people, but he and I were in the same squadron before he got shot down and received his burns."

Lieutenant Colonel Sloan looked somewhat surprised at that information.

"Somehow you always seem to surprise me, Major Haynes," Sloan said after a moment.

"Sir, I still technically own a Queen's commission," Adam said somberly. "It's not like I've never flown a *Spitfire*."

"You've already thought this out, haven't you?" Sloan asked cynically.

"Not really, but I'm not letting some yahoo who has never been shot at a day in his life toss me in the stockade for telling the truth. I came here to kill Germans, period."

"Just why do you hate them so much?" Sloan asked, looking up as VMF-21's *Wildcats* started their engines.

"Sir, sometime when we have time and alcohol I'll tell you the story," Adam said, "but for now we've got to get moving."

"Just one more thing: Why are you so confident he won't come back?" Sloan asked quickly, stopping Adam just as he started to turn away.

"Because a 109," Adam said, referring to the *Luftwaffe*'s older fighter, "will beat a *Warhawk* above 10,000 feet. A Focke Wulf 190 will beat anything besides a *Spitfire* nine times out of ten. Perry will run into one of the two today after staying around trying to play the hero, then he's going to get a chest full of German metal and a free ticket to Hell."

"So what makes you so sure we'll be coming back?" Sloan asked, half-joking. Adam could see that the man was starting to have doubts.

Good, that means he's been listening, Adam thought. Which is good, because I've got the more combat time than anyone else on this airfield.

"I know *I* am coming back because my squadron will not when the German fighters arrive. Even if they do arrive earlier than we thought, we all know the Thach Weave and we're more maneuverable than them."

"You have a lot of faith in Commander Thach's tactics," Sloan responded.

"He survived Sandwich Islands and Wake," Adam responded. "The *Wildcat* can out turn all the German fighters even if it can't outrun them. Once we teach some

Experten to be cautious by shooting a few of them in the face, they'll give us space to dive away."

"Can't they catch us in a dive?" Sloan asked, genuinely curious.

"The *Wildcat* can out dive anything besides a falling cement truck, and I add that qualifier only because no one's dropped a cement truck from twenty thousand feet to see," Adam replied. The sound of releasing brakes brought his head around, and he watched as Captain Cobb began leading his flight out towards the runway.

Cobb needs to get a squadron of his own soon, Adam thought, then turned back to Sloan. He obviously saw Sloan has hung me up and took the initiative to get things moving on his own.

"Sir, just remember not to hang around at height, and trust in Captain Zeda to keep you alive."

"Suddenly I'm glad that I chose a Buccaneer to be my wingman," Sloan said grimly. Adam nodded, recognizing the statement as the respect it was.

"Thanks, and good hunting, Sir," Adam replied. Coming to attention, Adam saluted his superior officer. Returning the gesture, Sloan turned to board his own fighter.

I hope he makes it back, Adam thought.

Morton Ranch
1345 Local
23 December 1965

"I never knew you had such a high opinion of me," Sam observed, his voice genuinely shocked.

"Yeah, well, I thought you would have made a better commander for the Black Knights than that poor bastard Bonnay," Adam said. He turned before Tabitha could ask the question. "Major Bonnay was a good man and a good pilot. The man just lacked situational awareness, and it eventually killed him."

"I read Mr. Caidin's book," Tabitha said. "You never mentioned half of these opinions in it."

"Remember he was writing an anthology," Adam replied. "He asked about the second half of the American Air Expeditionary Force's time in the Soviet Union, not the first."

"Why has no one written about the first half?" Tabitha asked.

"Because you'd need a gypsy to find anyone willing to talk about it," Jeff said sarcastically, his voice barely loud enough for Tabitha and Jacob to hear. "You're lucky my father obviously loves Jo."

"Let's concentrate on the matter at hand or we'll be here all day," Jacob said, looking at the clock. "I'm sure you'll have plenty of time to pick Mr. Haynes and your uncle's brains later."

"Fine," Tabitha said. She paused the tape, then rewound it a few minutes. "Okay, so this is what Wing Commander O'Rourke said was happening about the time you were taking off."

York Leader

Point Wellington (100 miles west of Moscow)
1110 Local
23 December 1943

While I realize this plan is simple because the Russians are involved, Wing Commander Connor O'Rourke thought to himself, *it is disturbingly similar to what we tried during the Second Battle of Britain. We all know how that turned out.*

Tall and wiry, Connor had plenty of room in the *Spitfire's* cockpit to turn around and look at his assembled wing. With the oxygen mask rubbing against the burn scars that covered the lower half of his face, he fought the urge to loosen its straps. The thirty-one other shark-like fighters were stepped back behind him in pairs, the new Mk IXs tasked with the job of stripping the German fighter escort from their bombers so the Americans and Russians had a fighting chance.

Last time I did this was when I got my lovely scars, Connor thought with a slight bit of apprehension. *I'd prefer to keep the rest of me from getting well done, so I hope the boffins are right about this kite being a game changer.*

Despite retaining its famous predecessor's long, lean lines and rounded elliptical wings, the Mark IX was a much different *Spit*. By adding 25% more horsepower, fixing the carburetors so that the engine did not cut out under 'negative-g', and changing the armament to four 20mm cannons, the manufacturers claimed to have matched the speed and firepower of the Focke-Wulf.

At least ol' Jerry won't be able to tell us apart until we're already mixed up. That should be a swell surprise for several of them, Connor mused. Looking out over his starboard wing, he saw several formations of Russian Lend-Lease Spitfires in the distance.

I guess adding those ducks quacking with a Russian accent will help in the subterfuge, Connor thought with gallows humor. *Poor bastards are flying Lend-Lease Mark IIs, and that's going to be a massacre.*

"York Leader, tallyho, many bandits, eleven o'clock low!" a calm voice sounded in his ear. Connor looked slightly to the left and down, seeing the gaggle of hostile Germans below. There was at least thirty of the enemy, and he watched as they began to turn towards his fighters.

Here goes, Connor thought.

"Righto, I've got them. Kestrel Squadron, high cover! Harrier, Eagle, follow me!" Connor barked, shoving his throttle forward to the maximum and diving towards the Germans. Out of the corner of his eye he saw many more aircraft approaching from the east.

Bloody hell, the Russians are indeed going 'all in,' Connor thought.

Then it was time to pay attention to matters at hand, namely the rapidly swelling Focke-Wulf 190 in his sight. Connor had chosen the leader of the approaching enemy flight, his height giving him a temporary advantage over his opponent. The 190 was a bulky, brutish-looking aircraft, with a round, radial engine as opposed to the *Spitfire*'s inline. Watching the exhaust smoke pouring from the engine, Connor felt a moment's sympathy for the hapless German before firing a quick burst as he descended. There were several bright flashes on the 190's fuselage, then he was kicking the rudder and moving his stick to pass through the German formation. Once through the snarling 190s and the couple of tracer rounds some hopeful German pilot had lofted at him, he pulled back on his stick to zoom climb while looking for another target.

"Red Four, look out!"

Connor turned his head back to his right just in time to see an explosion and debris as a *Spit* and 190 collided to his left rear. Muttering an oath as he whipped his head around, he saw that the German leader was already rolling and re-orienting towards him. Used to facing the slower climbing *Spitfire* Mark Vs, the German suddenly found himself hanging like ripe fruit a little more than a football pitch's length away from Connor's fighter.

More's the pity, Connor thought as he closed to make sure of his burst.

"Get him York Leader, his wingman's out of the fight," Connor's wingman said. The German pilot had just enough time to try and half-roll so he could dive away before Connor fired, the burst walking from nose to tail, shattering the canopy and blowing the tail structure off on the way.

"Break left, York Leader" his wingman grunted. Connor didn't even look to see why the man gave his warning, tightening his turn and again reapplying throttle. As the g-forces forced his vision to a tight tunnel, he saw two 190s that had attempted to bounce him going past in a dive. Showing that they were veteran pilots, both Germans continued on their dives to gain separation from the *Spitfires*.

Never get into a phone booth with a knife fighter, Connor thought, adding throttle to chase the two Germans.

"Get him off me, get him off me!" Connor heard someone shout, the scream making him suddenly aware the radio net was alive with traffic. Recognizing the voice as one of the new flight lieutenants from 345 "Eagle" Squadron, Connor cursed as the lad started screaming in a high pitched, keening voice that stopped abruptly.

That's at least one boxing job tonight, he thought grimly. One only had to hear a man screaming in agony as he burned to death once to recognize the sound. Swiveling his head, he saw that the two 190s had snap-rolled to change their direction of flight and were now coming back around.

"Cagey bastards there," Connor remarked over the radio. "Head on run, York Two," Connor said.

The two Germans and their British counterparts hurtled towards each other, firing once they got into range. Connor was uncomfortably aware of several tracers going by his canopy. There was a sharp bang followed by his fighter skidding to the left as his port cannon stopped firing. Before Connor could curse, he watched as the skid took his line of fire right through his assailant's flight path. Shedding pieces, the Fw-190 hurtled by just over his head, white smoke starting to pour out behind it as the pilot rolled and dived away. Glancing to his left side for his wingman, Connor saw that the other 190 was a ball of flame arcing down towards the steppes below.

"Good shooting York Two!" he barked.

"Roger, York Leader," his wingman gasped. "But he wasn't that bad a shot himself."

"Right, let's get you down from here," Connor said. Looking at his watch, he realized barely three minutes had passed since his initial dive.

All right you Colonials, we've done our part now you do yours, Connor thought as he followed the smoking York Two back towards the east.

Morton Ranch
1410 Local
23 December 1945

"Poor bastard died that night," Adam observed, referring to York Two. "He'd taken too many fragments, had internal bleeding."

Tabitha gave a short sound of surprise at that.

"How was he able to land the plane?" Jeff asked.

"Blood loss isn't as quick as people think," Adam replied. "Often a pilot with just a few fragments in him or one to two bullets in him wouldn't realize how badly he was hurt. Otherwise they would have set down as quickly as possible rather than keep trying to fly home."

"But I thought they were still over German lines?" Tabitha asked, gesturing towards where Jeff was opening *Bomber Pilot for the Reich* to read the next index card.

"Would you rather be a live prisoner for a couple of years or be free for the last thirty minutes of your life?" Adam asked simply. "If I'd been as badly shot up as York Two was, I would have put her down near a town."

"Why not bail out?" Jeff inquired.

"Because you can bleed to death by the time someone gets to where you landed in your parachute," Adam responded.

"Oh." There was an awkward silence before Tabitha motioned for the younger Haynes to read the next section.

"I apologize if my translation is slightly off," Jeff said, then began reading from *Bomber Pilot for the Reich*.

Oberst Stephen Häas looked at the swirling fighting around his He-111 and felt his chest grow tight with a mingling of joy, awe, and excitement. The Moscow run had been frightening initially, the Russians throwing up a desperate defense that included dense anti-aircraft fire and numerous fighters. Then there had been roughly four days of few interceptors, an event that had seemed ominous. Now, however, it appeared that the Russians had thrown their maximum strength at the attacking German bombers.

It just shows how desperate the Bolsheviks are, Stephen thought to himself. *Soon we will burn out the beast's heart, and that will be the end of the final threat to an Aryan Europe*. With his blonde hair, blue eyes, and rugged build, Stephen could have been the poster child for National Socialism. Despite this, he had begun the war apolitical. Now, Germany's continued victories had almost made him a full believer.

"We will be reaching our initial point in another fifteen minutes, Oberst," his bombardier-gunner, *Hauptmann* Johann Düttman said. The initial point was the location where they would begin their bomb run, thereafter maintaining a straight and level heading so that Johann could hit the Moscow rail station that was their ostensible target. In reality, the He-111's internal bomb bay caused the bombs to often scatter wildly, meaning they could only guarantee that they would hit something in Moscow.

There was another explosion followed by a long, trailing smoke trail above and to port. The destroyed fighter was too far away for Stephen to identify it.

"It appears intelligence was correct when they said this would bring the rats out of their dens," Johann observed.

"No matter, the *Jagdflieger* appear to be giving them all they can handle and more," Stephen replied.

"I bet the boys in the back of the formation wish they could be up here to see this," Johann crowed, pointing as another flaming comet fell out of the sky to starboard. The Luftwaffe, in order to make the jobs of the escorting fighters easier, had begun placing the He-111s in the front of the formation since they were slower than the Ju-88s.

"It is just like Spain all over again," Stephen said, a rare smile crossing his face. He and Johann had been comrades since that war, both still wearing their Condor Legion badges for good luck.

"Or Britain," one of their gunners, *Obergefreiter* Adolf Jaeger, chimed in. He was stationed behind the two pilots in the He-111's dorsal turret. Stephen and Johann rolled their eyes at each other, making non-committal grunts over the intercom. Adolf had only been with their crew a short time, his predecessor having been selected for transfer to a newly forming heavy bomber unit. No one cared for him, least of all Stephen.

The man does not know his place, Stephen thought.

"Achtung, *Spitfire*," someone cried over the radio. A cold fear gripped both of the men in the bomber's nose as they both looked around to see where the attacking fighter was approaching from.

"I see him!" Johann said, his tone urgent as he followed up the statement by turning the cannon to starboard. Stephen turned to see the attacking fighter as well, the Russian *Spitfire* curving back around to make another run after having missed with his first run. The three He-111s in *KG*

74's lead flight began hosing fire at the approaching fighter, their tracers arcing alla round the nimble *Spit*. For his part, the Russian pilot began returning fire, wings sparkling in a fashion that made Stephen bowels loosen as he watched Death coming right for him.

One moment the *Spitfire* was approaching. The next it was a wildly spinning bundle of debris, its starboard wing flying off in a sparkle of tracers that came almost straight down. A bright yellow Me-109 dived just in front of *KG* 74's lead flight a moment later, a few of the gunners shooting at it before they recognized the iron crosses on its flank. Stephen, on the other hand, recognized the pain scheme.

"General Mölders!" both pilot and bombardier shouted in exultation.

I thought Field Marshal Kesselring explicitly forbade him from flying any operational sorties over enemy territory, Stephen thought. He looked briefly over Johann's shoulder at their current position.

I guess he's technically observing the letter of the rule, but certainly not the spirit, Stephen thought. They watched as the 109 turned back towards the west far beneath them.

"Must be out of fuel," Stephen remarked.

"Or ammo," Johann added. "Lord knows they've probably used enough of it."

Indeed, as they looked around them, a sudden eerie calm appeared to have descended upon the skies, with no aircraft in sight besides their accompanying bombers. Stephen suddenly felt naked.

"*Zerstorers*, coming in above," Adolf reported as if on cue. Stephen felt a slight sense of relief. The twin-engined Me-210s weren't the best thing for escort, but they beat having to rely on their own light machine guns.

"Thank you," Stephen said.

"As usual, they are far too late to do anything, as it would appear that the Russian bastards have been taught the errors of their ways," Johann replied bitterly. "There probably isn't an enemy fighter within a hundred miles of us."

Chapter 4: Reaping and Saving

Morton Ranch
1445 Local
23 December 1965

"Sorry, I should have realized everyone needed a bathroom break," Tabitha said to her mother as the two of them washed their hands in one of the main house's bathrooms.

"Yeah, guess my frantic hand signals weren't seen," Jo observed dryly. "Good thing you heard the clink of my teeth as they started to float."

"Moooommm," Tabitha replied as they stepped out into Jacob's master bedroom. "No need to be dramatic."

A picture caught Jo's eye just as they were about to leave the room. Turning, she was shocked to see it was her wedding picture. Her slight gasp caught Tabitha's attention, and she turned to look as well.

"Oh," Tabitha said.

"What do you mean, oh?" Jo asked, her voice still slightly breathless.

"I thought you knew Granddad still had that picture on his dresser," Tabitha said simply. "It's been there ever since I started visiting."

"No, I did not know Dad still had that picture," Jo said quietly. Looking at the faded black and white, she was suddenly struck by how she had looked so young yet so old at the same time.

War ages you in dog years, the older woman thought.

"I think I see why you and Adam get along so well," Tabitha observed.

"Why's that?" Jo asked.

"You both have demons, yet you don't pry," Tabitha replied evenly. "I have dozens of questions right now, but I know better than to ask you."

Jo sighed at the start of a frequent argument.

"It's not easy to talk about the past," Jo said guardedly.

"It's not easy growing up with ghosts you can never talk about either, Mom," Tabitha replied quietly, her tone without heat. Jo looked at her daughter and saw that the young lady was barely holding her tears in.

I'm so sorry, Jo thought.

"I never intended to keep that part away from you, Tabitha," Jo intoned after a moment. "It just hurts so much to talk about your father."

"Well Granddad only met him once at Aunt Patricia's wedding," Tabitha snapped. "If there's someone who makes *you* seem like a Gabby Abby about the war…"

Oh if only you understood just how hectic things were during the war, Jo thought. *Or if I told you I kept refusing to acknowledge my feelings for your father precisely because of what happened with your Aunt Patricia.*

"That's not fair to your Aunt Patricia," Jo said aloud, her voice stern. "Not even sorta. The woman started the war with four brothers, ended it with two, and was a widow to boot. You at least know what happened to your father—her husband is just another name on a memorial somewhere."

Tabitha took a deep breath.

"She won't even talk about Dad or Uncle David," Tabitha said. "It's like neither one of them ever existed."

Jo took Tabitha's hands in hers.

You have no idea how much it hurt her, Jo thought. *Your aunt used to be a happy, funny woman.*

"I promise, Tabitha, we will talk about your father. Not someday, but this week," Jo said. "It's past time."

"Jo, everyone's waiting on Tabitha," Jacob called down the hallway.

"On the way, Dad," Jo shouted back.

The two women entered the dining room to find that Jacob had not been exaggerating. Natalia shifted from where she'd been sitting talking quietly to Adam and Sam. She grabbed *Women for the Rodina!* and moved back to her chair.

"Well, guess it's time to hear from the Army," Sam observed.

"For what that's worth," Adam growled. Jo could see that her boyfriend was tense, his hands clasped tightly in front of him. Tabitha did not see the tension, her focus on the report in front of her.

"On 23 December 1943, the 12th Composite Wing, United States Army Air Force, engaged approximately thirty enemy bombers and an unknown number of fighters…"

Cardinals One
1122 Local
23 December 1943

"Let us…prey," Major Mark Price heard over his earphones. The sentence sounded intimate, almost whispered, and he had the feeling whomever had transmitted it had done so unintentionally.

Usually happens with these damn mask mikes, Price thought as he fought with his P-40F *Warhawk*. *No matter, it's certainly apt.* His brown hair was matted down under his helmet, and the edges of his mask dug into his cheeks. The adrenaline coursing through him prevented most of the cold at 22,000 feet from registering, and his green eyes scanned the sky looking for German fighters. Licking his lips, he looked forward at the two P-40Fs leading the formation, silently willing Colonel Perry to hurry up and give the order to attack. Below the gathered Americans, the grey Heinkels droned on in their vee of vees formation, the sun glinting off their dorsal turrets.

I don't know if that bastard Haynes is right or wrong, but mercenary or not he's got over a dozen scalps, Price thought. *Makes a man start to believe what he's saying.*

Price knew several of his fellow *Warhawk* pilots viewed the Marine as an asshole. However, as he felt his *Warhawk* struggling for power, it occurred to him the stocky Marine just might know what he was talking about with regards to high altitude fighting. Looking down and forward, Price saw the seemingly endless stream of German bombers with the Me-210s starting to weave above their charges.

Only a matter of time before those damn fighters see us, he thought grimly. *Or, better yet, actually realize we're not friendly.* From a distance the P-40 looked closed enough to the Me-109 to cause confusion, but every second the Americans lingered made it more likely some German gunner would realize he was looking at dark green aircraft rather than dark gray.

"Vipers," Colonel Perry said as if reading his mind, "you have the heavy fighters. Red Squadron, you take the lead vic of bombers, White the second, Blue the third. Green and Yellow, you will remain as top cover. Follow me!"

What in the Hell is he thinking? Price had time to think before he kicked his rudder. The "127th Pursuit Squadron, or "Vipers," were P-39Q *Airacobras*. The P-39's primary reason for existence was to destroy enemy bombers. While relatively nimble at low altitude, like the *Warhawk* it was very clumsy above 10,000 feet.

No time to think about that now, Price thought. Waggling his wings, he led the rest of his "Cardinals," as the 12th Pursuit Squadron was known, down into the attack. Selecting the lead Heinkel, Price made one last frantic check of his arming switches, then picked out the lead bomber.

Haynes said something about the leader usually having the best bombardier, Price thought, heart in his throat as the twin engine craft swelled in his gunsight. He was dimly aware of the 210s scattering like quail as they realized the incoming fighters were not friendly. The dorsal gunner on the He-111 belatedly opened fire, and time seemed to dilate as the stream of tracers began to swing towards his aircraft.

If he's in range, then obviously so am I, Price thought, mashing his trigger. His fighter vibrated violently as the six wing-mounted .50-caliber machine guns opened fire. The weapons' combined effect was horrible to behold. Like a ravenous animal worrying a bone, the burst ripped into the He-111's starboard fuselage and wing. He watched as debris flew off the bomber, the dorsal turret imploding as his burst walked forward towards the bomber's glass nose.

Stab Flight / Kampfgeschwader (KG) 74
40 miles west of Moscow
1124 Local
23 December 1943

One moment Stephen had been about to respond with a joke about Johann's comment there wasn't an enemy fighter within a hundred miles. The next, Adolf's screams were only drowned out by shattering glass and the sound of bullets passing through the Heinkel's cockpit. Miraculously, Stephen and Johann both survived the hornet's nest of bullets and shattering glass, instrument panel debris, and fragments from the nose gun's shattered breech. Cursing, Stephen struggled to control their damaged bomber, fuel and oil streaming back from their starboard wing.

What in the Hell just happened? Stephen thought to himself, thankful he was able to stop the skidding bomber from falling out of formation. Six of the surrounding Heinkels weren't so lucky, two exploding as bullets met high explosives or fuel tanks. The other four, smoking heavily, broke from formation while jettisoning their bombloads.

I hope they didn't just drop on friendly forces, Stephen thought. The savage attack had disrupted all of KG 74, and he watched as another He-111 burst into flames as more enemy fighters dove from above.

Where are the Zerstorers? Stephen thought.

Unbeknownst to Stephen, the *Zerstorers* had problems of their own in the form of the 127th Pursuit. While Colonel Perry had made a tactical error, the P-39s' armament functioned on the large Me-210s just as effectively as it would have on bombers. Caught while trying to slow down and form up on the He-111s, the twin-engine fighters never had a chance. Their leader barely had time to cry out a warning before a 37mm shell entered the cockpit and blew the man's seat armor through his torso and into the instrument panel. The Oberst was joined in death by two of his subordinates, with another two Me-210s sufficiently mauled they had to break off the battle.

A prewar comrade of Colonel Perry, the 127th Pursuit's squadron leader turned out of his dive and circled back to engage the Me-210s. Despite being outnumbered almost two to one by the surviving Me-210s, the 127th's pilots did not hesitate in following their commander around into the disorganized *Zerstorers*. For their part, the shaken Germans put themselves into a 'Lufberry' circle, a defensive maneuver that had each of the big fighters chasing the tail of another. While ensuring the P-39s were presented with extremely difficult targets, the maneuver did nothing for the horribly vulnerable He-111s other than ensure they were wholly unprotected.

Buccaneer One
40 miles west of Moscow
1126 Local
23 December 1943

Nice bounce, Army pukes, Adam thought appreciatively as he turned to port and oriented his nose ahead of the German bombers. Approaching from the north, he had seen the P-40s and P-39s initiate their assault. Even as he watched, most of the Army fighters were circling to the south and clearing the way for their USMC counterparts. Several P-40s broke off to go aid the P-39s, and it appeared the Me-210s were about to have their circle cut apart. Impatient, two of the *Airacobras* didn't wait for the *Warhawks* to arrive, believing they could strike at a target before the next set of Me-210s brought their weapons to bear. It almost worked, but in exchange for getting a piece of a Me-210 the lead *Airacobra* ran right into fire from two other *Zerstorers'* nose armament.

Yep, looks like those boys figured ol' Major Haynes was an idiot, Adam thought. *Tried to warn them what the 210s would do, but no one wanted to listen to me.*

Then it was time for his attack.

"Red Flight, follow me," Adam said, rocking his wings and diving back to starboard after the He-111s. Unlike the Army pilots, the Marines had not formed one massive wing. Instead, the three squadron commanders had decided to hit at different points among the bomber stream, attempting to force multiple squadrons to break away from Moscow as well as make the escorts' job much harder. Adam had seen big wings during the Second Battle of Britain, and the idea worked a lot better on paper than in execution.

The first four *Wildcats* followed Adam down as he came in from above and forward of the He-111s. With their high closing speed and angle, the Marines would only have a few moments to shoot, but what shots hit were bound to do far more damage coming from forward.

We'll definitely know who can put lead on target after this, Adam thought, taking a deep breath from his oxygen mask. The He-111s seemed to leap into range, and he squeezed the trigger on his stick.

Current Marine doctrine had stated that machine guns should be boresighted to converge at three hundred yards. Rather than follow that guidance, Adam had boresighted his guns at an absurdly close range of one hundred meters. While his machine guns could and did shoot far beyond that, that measurement was the point where all six streams would put their bullets into a space smaller than the average fighter. The impact of so many bullets in such a small space was like a giant buzz saw as it slashed into the front of the He-111. Johann never knew what hit him, dying in a spray of gore that covered Stephen's flight tunic. The burst continued on to smash the starboard engine into junk, then weakened the wing sufficiently that the slipstream caused it to rip off the bomber. Adam kicked his rudder and passed underneath the mortally wounded He-111, noting the wild and inaccurate tracers arcing by his fighter from the surrounding KG 74 gunners.

Buccaneer Five
40 miles west of Moscow
1127 Local
23 December 1943

For his part, Sam had swung his flight wide to attack the fourth section of Heinkels from the Germans' port rear. Seeing Adam's handiwork spinning down out of the formation, Sam hoped that Red Flight had drawn most of the gunners' attention. Taking a quick glance off his wing, he saw David was tucked in tight.

"Let's go, White Flight," Sam said, shaking the stick back and forth then pushing over. With the engine racing in front of him, he watched as the He-111 began to swell in his sight. Unfortunately, the shock effect of Red Flight's attack wore off just as White Flight was getting into firing range. As the lead fighter, Sam drew the majority of the surviving Germans' fire. The sound of slugs bouncing off the big engine and wings in front of him caused him to jerk, skidding the *Wildcat* before he brought it back under control. Time suddenly seemed to triple its normal speed as he felt a killing rage descend upon him.

You motherfuckers! he thought, peering through his sight. The He-111's gunner blazed desperately at him, the heavy machine gun tracers streaking by the *Wildcat*'s cockpit. So close he could make out the man's features, Sam squeezed the trigger and watched the gunner blown back into the fuselage, then his bullets move forward until they blew out the nose in a gout of glass and debris. Desperately kicking his rudder, Sam passed just in front of his target. Checking his rearview mirror, he saw the big Heinkel ablaze, flames filling the cockpit area like some infernal greenhouse.

Got you, you bast…

The explosion seemed to turn all the sound in the world back on, glass slamming into his left shoulder and jaw with a white-hot lancing pain while shell fragments stung the back of his right hand on the stick. Ignoring the pain and suddenly glad he had remembered to lower his goggles, Sam fought for control of the *Wildcat* as several more hits registered on the tubby fighter's fuselage.

Damn ventral gunners, he thought as the FM-2 began to spin downwards. Fighting the stick, he brought the fighter back under control. Cold air was already starting to numb his hands as he fought to bring the nose back up.

"White Leader, White Leader, are you all right?!" David's cries broke through the cacophony of the squadron net. Sam looked at his shoulder, seeing a nasty, jagged cut just above his unit patch. Moving the arm, he realized that it was quite stiff, but that he would be all right.

Holy shit, it did that through my jacket! he realized. Listening to the rush of air, he realized that the entire left side of his cockpit glass was gone.

"I'm fine, White Two," Sam reassured his brother. "I have to drop down to angels ten, I just lost my canopy."

"Clear the net you idiots, you can celebrate when we get home!"

Major Haynes roaring voice brought some quiet to the net. Moving the stick to come back to level flight, Sam realized the *Wildcat*'s engine was running slightly rough. As the little fighter vibrated, he tried to peer forward to see just how bad the damage was.

"White Two, how does my plane look," Sam asked, exasperated.

"Like it was shot up by a bunch of angry Germans!" David replied sardonically, making him want to reach out and box his twin's ears.

"All flights break off, all flights break off! Bandits, coming in from the west! All Buccaneers return to base!" Haynes barked.

"White One, roger!" Sam responded, followed quickly by all the flight leaders except for Green.

"Green One, Green One, respond!" Haynes barked. "Any Green element, respond now!"

Sam could hear the anger in the squadron leader's voice.

Someone's in for an ass chewing of epic proportions if they don't get on the radio, Sam thought.

"This is Green Two, Green One is down, Green Flight headed for base," came a slightly tremulous voice.

Shit, Sam thought with a shiver that had nothing to do with the cold air slamming into his cockpit.

Guess someone had to be the first to die, he thought. As he brought the blue *Wildcat* around towards Moscow, motion to his front right caught his attention.

Morton Ranch
1530 Local
23 December 1965

"I get the feeling you were not upset to see this Captain Bowles did not make it back," Natalia observed flatly.

"Couldn't have happened to a more useless guy," Adam insisted evenly.

"I knew his father," Jacob said quietly. "Admiral Bowles was a real asshole but his wife was a wonderful woman. I'm not sure she deserved to lose her son as well as her husband."

"Her son diddled another man's wife, assaulted me, constantly questioned my authority, and basically behaved like the untouchable prick he was right up until time came to see the elephant," Adam snapped.

"Did they ever figure out why Captain Bowles did not come back?" Tabitha queried.

"The Soviets found his fighter when they counterattacked in January," Adam replied. "Some German gunner put a twenty millimeter shell through his windshield and damn near decapitated him."

Tabitha gulped at Adam's response, and he felt Jo squeeze his hand.

Your daughter doesn't want to be treated like a delicate flower, I'm going to tell it to her straight.

"I see," Tabitha replied.

"Why didn't you have Sam's brother take over Green Flight when you got to Russia?" Jeff asked. "Seems like no one would have told you different."

"David and I were a package deal," Sam said tersely. "We'd been together since the womb and it had worked out so far. He didn't want to…"

To Adam's shock, the big man's voice trailed off as emotion caught up with him. Natalia quickly stood and wrapped her arms around her husband as Sam's shoulders shook. Turning, Adam was surprised to see tears glistening in Jo's eyes as well. Adam reached over and hugged Jo towards him, the woman fiercely hugging him back.

I can still remember both of you big idiots walking into the diner outside Tacoma, Adam thought, surprised to find his own eyes starting to burn.

"I think we're going to need a few minutes," he said to Tabitha. The young woman nodded, then looked at the coffee pot.

"I'll make some more coffee," she said.

"I'll help," Jeff chimed in, his voice clearly uncomfortable. The two teenagers quickly left the room, leaving both couples with a pensive Jacob. After a moment, the former admiral stood and followed the teens into the kitchen.

"Thinking about the war is like opening Pandora's box," Jo said softly to Adam as he rubbed her back. "You think you're going to just let one thing out, but all the sudden there are memories, both good and bad, everywhere."

"Just like everyone's favorite curious Greek maiden, I don't think your daughter understood what she was unleashing," Adam observed.

"I promised her I'd tell her about her father," Jo said. Adam stiffened despite himself.

"You don't think that's a good idea," Jo observed quietly.

"I know what it takes out of you," Adam replied. "You had nightmares for two weeks straight after you told me your backstory."

He felt Jo make a face against his chest.

"Is that why you don't talk much about your past?" she asked quietly. Adam took a deep breath. "You're afraid you'll get nightmares?"

"No," Adam replied. "It's because unlike Pandora I know a good welder," Adam said. Jo leaned back and was about to say something when Sam interrupted them.

"Sorry about that," Sam drawled, dabbing his eyes with a handkerchief.

"You may notice the only dry eyes in the house are Russian," Adam observed, grinning to prove he meant no ill will towards Natalia. The comely woman shrugged.

"I have not yet had enough vodka to cry properly," she said, the slight tremble in her voice belying her words. "Besides, I wail like an old woman, and no one deserves to hear that."

All three adults were laughing when Tabitha came back in, carrying the metal coffee urn with a pair of potholders. She looked at the four adults like they'd lost their minds.

"Granddad and Jeff went to go grab some firewood," she announced. "Granddad said you guys would need it in the guest house tonight."

Uh oh, Adam thought. That could be either a good thing or a bad thing. Wonder if there's a 'talk' going on?

"You have a strange look on your face, Mr. Haynes," Tabitha noted.

"He's wondering if your grandfather's about to chop your boy…I mean, his son, in half," Sam muttered. Tabitha whirled to look at Sam.

"He is *not* my boyfriend," Tabitha countered indignantly.

"Who's not your boyfriend?" Jacob asked as he walked into the room, Jeff right behind him. The younger Haynes looked at Tabitha, his face slightly crestfallen.

"No one! No one's my boyfriend," Tabitha shrilled. Jeff's face brightened for a moment before he tried to regain a poker countenance.

Oh no, son, not that easy, Adam thought with a wicked smile. *Not after how you've acted today*.

"Well I suppose Jeff is quite happy to hear that," Adam observed, the comment eliciting several guffaws from the gathered adults. Jeff, his face almost as red as his hair, turned to look at Adam in shock.

"So, we will now hear from the Russians!" Tabitha declared emphatically, her own face redder than normal.

With a slight smile, Natalia picked up *Women for the Rodina!* and began to read.

"Comrade Tochenova was aloft on the day of the German defeat. Like most of her regiment, she had been assigned to fly at low altitude to pick off German stragglers…"

Rook One
1130 Local
23 December 1943

Valeria Tochenova was not having a good day. A tall, slender woman with long brunette hair, the provisional Red Air Force Major had started the day as the executive officer of the newly formed 332nd Fighter Regiment. The 332nd had been ordered to take its Yak-1s and attack the back of the German bomber stream once the escort was engaged by Americans and Commonwealth fighters. The plan had worked quite well until German reinforcements had shown up, at which point the fight had degenerated into a wild free for all. Twelve thousand feet, two kills, a dead regimental commander, and one missing wingman later, Valeria had quietly resolved never to underestimate German fighters again. Judging by what she had already seen, if the day ended with seven of her fellow women alive, it would be a minor miracle.

We'll be lucky if half of us make it home today, Valeria thought. *If I do not think of something quickly, the dead will include me.*

The distant dot she had seen off her starboard wing had begun arcing around to her rear, then started closing. Looking at the plane, the Russian officer recognized it as a Me-109 beginning its attack run. Waiting until the last moment, Valeria desperately kicked her rudder pedals, skidding the damaged Yak-1 to starboard. She had timed her evasion well, the burst of tracer fire just missing her as the Me-109 swinging far too wide to get a good bead on her. If her engine had not been making ominous noises or her fighter not drawing a finger of smoke across the sky, Valeria would have snap rolled onto the Messerchmitt's tail.

PANDORA'S MEMORIES

At least my opponent appears to be a poor pilot, Valeria mused with hot anger. *I'm damaged and he still managed to miss me. Were this plane whole, I would have gotten on his tail and shot him down right there.*

As if angered by her mental assessment, the German pilot reversed course and came in firing once more. This time her skid did not fully work, as a cannon shell banged into her engine, the propeller windmilling to a stop as black oil coated the windscreen.

So this is how it ends, Valeria thought. *I kill two of the Fascists bastards and then get murdered by a third.* She desperately looked for a place to land as the 109 lazily turned in for the coup de grace.

I don't know why I'm trying to crash land, she thought grimly. The war in the air, like that on the ground, knew no quarter. Even if she crash-landed, the German would probably come back around and strafe her before she could get away through the endless drifts. Nonetheless, Valeria saw an open field to her front and lined the steadily more sluggish Yak up with it. Moments later, the long nose plunged down in a huge plume of snow and oil. White agony slammed through her as the impact crushed her chest against the seat straps, eliciting a scream of pain. With nausea swirling her stomach, she struggled to unclip herself from the seat, cursing male designers with every tortured breath.

Getting the canopy open, she heard the roar of the 109's engine as it lined up on her.

Now he kills me, she thought helplessly. Reflecting on her life, Valeria realized the irony behind the one thing she had always enjoyed killing her. Dropping into a ball in her canopy, waiting for the executioner's axe to fall, Valeria realized what a fool she had been to push so hard for the privilege of flying in combat.

Dammit, all the men will say they were right and that this was no place for a woman…

Buccaneer Five
40 miles west of Moscow
1135 Local
23 December 1943

Does that idiot not see us? Sam thought incredulously. The 109 had circled the downed Yak twice before lining up on what looked like a textbook strafing run. The whole time, Sam and David had been desperately closing, hoping to arrive in time to save the white painted Soviet.

For fuck's sake, we're flying in freakin' dark blue fighters, Sam thought. *Either he doesn't think we can hit a deflection shot or he has badly misjudged the range.*

With that, Sam applied lead to account for the 109's high speed and shallow dive. The range was so close by the time he fired that the German pilot was clearly visible. At the last moment, it appeared the German realized his danger, as the pilot turned his head towards Sam. Then the *Wildcat* was shuddering from its machine guns, the 109 zooming right through the four streams of machine gun fire. What entered as a high performance fighter exited the far side of Sam's tracers as a falling ball of fire that passed maybe two hundred feet over the downed Yak. Pulling back on his own stick, Sam ignored the falling fighter and checked the air around them.

"That's two!" David crowed.

Yes, but let's make sure he didn't have a wingman, Sam thought

Sam turned to see the column of black smoke that had been the German fighter and, beyond it, several men starting to rush out of a group of nearby buildings. Completing a circle, Sam passed over the men and the downed aircraft, waggling his wings. The men, rifles clearly in their hands, did not wave back at the dark blue aircraft with their strange white stars.

"Let's get out of here, I'm low on fuel," Sam said, looking at his gauge. *That and this air is starting to give me frostbite.* Despite the cold, he felt a smile cross his face.

Good thing I have great peripheral vision, he thought. I think some Russian is going to have to bring me his vodka ration.

Rook 1

Valeria leaned up against her fighter and watched as the two planes flew off into the distance. Turning her head to the side, she saw where the German 109 continued to burn.

I did not think Ratas moved that fast, she said. *Or that anyone was still flying them.* Looking closer, she realized that the two departing aircraft could not be portly, obsolete I-16s. At that point, a blur of brown fur flying around the tail of her fighter with suspicious barks brought her attention back to the here and now. As the dog circled, its barks becoming increasingly high pitched, Valeria saw the group of men approaching on snowshoes. Seeing the red stars on her fuselage, the group lowered their rifles.

"Comrade, are you…" the nearest man called, then stopped as Valeria removed her helmet to wipe the cold sweat off of her brow. He stopped, mouth agape as her hair flopped down to her shoulders.

Come now, I know you are not captivated by my beauty, Valeria thought churlishly.

"Yes, I am a woman and yes, I am all right," she responded. The man's reaction made her temper rise, the old villager stepping back as if she was Baba Yaga made flesh.

Stupid idiot is probably shocked to see that a woman is good for something besides warming beds, food, or the backsides of children, Valeria thought bitterly. *The Party would be so proud.*

"I need to talk to the chairman of your collective, so I can see about getting this fighter moved," Valeria commanded. "If you are him, then please gather some horses and more men! If we leave this fighter here, someone *will* come by and shoot it."

"Comrade, why didn't those two other aircraft shoot at you? They had strange lettering on the side and a white star. What does it mean?" the villager asked.

"I do not know, but they saved my life and are shooting at the Germans…that is all I care for now," Valeria snapped.

Chapter 5: Fallen Comrades

Morton Ranch
1630 Local
23 December 1965

Tabitha stopped the tape recorder and gave both Sam and Adam a withering look. The two men were laughing uproariously at the last line Natalia had just uttered.

"What is so funny?" she asked archly. "We were just talking about Uncle Sam nearly getting killed!"

Adam and Sam both managed to stop laughing, their eyes noticeably wet.

"You had to know Valeria," Sam said, shaking his head.

"That line is so much like her," Adam replied. "An alien could step off a huge flying saucer it had just crash landed through an orphanage, but as long as the first person it shot with the Buck Rogers ray gun was German then Valeria would not care."

"'Pity those children had to die for the cause of killing Fascists,'" Sam said in a mock, falsetto Russian accent. Adam, having just gotten control of himself, started to laugh again.

"Sounds like someone else I know," Jo remarked wryly. Adam looked at her across the table, his laughter dying in this throat.

"Come to think of it, Valeria and you did get along rather well," Sam said playfully, causing Adam to turn and give him an almost identical gaze.

"Just how well?" Jo asked.

Uh oh, Adam thought, seeing Jeff's face as the young man started paying closer attention. *Let's nip this discussion in the bud.*

"Well enough that we're not going to talk about it," Adam said shortly, the tone of his voice quite clear. There was an awkward silence as Jo started to open her mouth, then closed it.

"So you said something earlier about an Army counterpart?" Jeff asked quickly. Looking at Jo, Adam could see his son's gambit was only partially successful.

"In all seriousness, I had started to date your mother already," Adam said somberly. "Valeria quickly found eyes for another man."

Not that it wasn't a near run thing, he thought.

"We're not here to find out about who dated who," Tabitha insisted, pinching Jeff. The young man gave a surprised yelp, then turned to pinch her back. With a nimbleness that surprised Adam, the young woman dodged, causing Jeff to unbalance himself in his chair. Arms flailing, the younger Haynes went over backwards. Once she saw he was okay, Tabitha started giggling at the young man, offering him a hand up. Once more red faced, Jeff took it and stood his chair up.

"Yes, speaking of Major Price," Tabitha said, turning back to Adam. The laughter dying in his chest, Adam took a deep breath.

"I think," Adam said slowly, "that's a story for another time."

"Wha..? Dad!" Jeff said. "C'mon, knowing you, there won't be another time."

Adam turned to look at his son, and Jeff almost physically slid back. Gaining control of his emotions, the former Buccaneer One clasped his hands in front of him and looked down at the map.

"There are times when you should let someone keep their thoughts to themselves, son," Adam said quietly, his voice clipped.

"Mr. Haynes, it'd be very helpful if you could tell me what happened," Tabitha pressed gently.

"Tabitha, the short version is that the Army suffered severe losses, which is why Major Price had time on his hands," Sam replied. Looking at his niece, he could tell that she was disappointed at his response. Sighing, he looked over at Adam.

"You want to tell the story or should I? Because I showed up later than you did."

"I guess I can," Adam said resignedly. "We had only been down on the ground for a few minutes…"

Moscow #6 North
1155 Local
23 December 1943

Adam pushed back his canopy and felt the cold December wind immediately begin clawing at his sweat-soaked frame.

Son-of-a-bitch that's cold, he thought to himself, shivering.

"Here you go, Sir," an orderly said from just behind the cockpit, startling him. The man was shoving a steaming cup in his hand. Adam took it, recognizing it for something that was supposed to be chicken soup.

"Thanks Sergeant MacDonald," Adam said, suddenly weary. Looking down the flight line, he could see the rest of the *Buccaneers* hopping out of their *Wildcat*s or gathering around those of the most recent returnees. Doing a quick count, he realized there were three of the tubby F4Fs missing. Downing the soup in a single gulp, he forced himself to his feet.

I'm getting too old for this crap, Adam thought. As he hit the ground, there was a faint sound of incoming engines. Shielding his eyes, he looked towards the west.

"So, looks like your brood did extremely well!" Lieutenant Colonel Sloan said, startling Adam with a slap on the back. Turning, Adam saw that his superior officer had obviously been busy himself.

"How'd the rest of the wing do, Sir?" Adam asked.

"Very good…oh my God!" Sloan started, his face suddenly becoming ashen as he looked past Adam. Adam whipped around, his body already starting to step towards his aircraft as the sound of approaching engines suddenly got louder. Looking up, he saw several approaching dots, one of them trailing a clearly visible streamer of black smoke. Squinting, Adam recognized the burning fighter as a P-40.

"Bail out you stupid bastard," Adam muttered. "You're not going to make it."

As if he heard Adam's admonishment, the *Warhawk* pilot inverted his fighter. All of the onlookers could see flames licking back from the Allison engine, playing around the canopy as the pilot opened it. The Marines cheered as the man kicked out of his aircraft and immediately deployed his chute, the white silk popping open several hundred feet above the ground. Their cheers suddenly became sounds of horror.

Oh Jesus, freakin' risers are on fire, Adam thought, fighting back the urge to vomit. The pilot had waited just a little too long before jumping out, and the fire had apparently spread to his parachute back. Adam turned away, having seen this particular scene play out before. The shouts and curses of the gathered Marines told him when the parachute collapsed, leaving the pilot to fall to his doom.

"Dammit," Sloan muttered, his voice a near sob. Adam shook his head as an ambulance rolled out from between two hangars at the end of the runway, siren screaming as it sped off towards the edge of the airfield where the pilot had come to earth.

I don't think you boys need to rush, he thought grimly. *Gravity's been winning against pilots since the Wright Brothers.*

"Where are the rest of them?" someone asked. "Where's the rest of the Army?"

Adam fought down the urge to laugh maniacally.

I have an idea where they are, he thought angrily. *Looks like some men should have listened to me.*

The remaining Army fighters broke into a landing pattern, their wings whistling from the airflow over their machine guns as they passed overhead. Taking a quick count of *Warhawks* and *Airacobras*, Adam realized that things were somewhat better than he had thought.

Still, at least five or six of those things are wrecks, he thought. As if on cue, one of the landing P-40s began to drift towards the side of the runway, obviously out of control. Before the pilot could react, the fighter's starboard wheel ran off the tarmac, causing the wing to dig into the turf and whip the fighter around in a vicious ground loop. With a crash, the fighter went through a tumbling routine that culminated with it upside down, with a wingtip flipping end over end across the grass.

"Did you see Colonel Perry's aircraft?" Sloan asked. The Army commander's P-40 had been adorned with a distinctive red band around the aft fuselage.

"No Sir, did not," Adam said.

"Come with me, Major," Sloan said, suddenly aware that there were several of the Marine pilots starting to migrate within ear shot. The two men began walking towards the Army flight line, Adam having to walk quite rapidly to keep up with his taller superior. As they strolled, Adam could see the wheels turning in Sloan's head.

If Perry is dead, that makes Sloan senior man, Adam mused to himself. *Poor bastard's probably wondering what he did to deserve this. No one likes battlefield promotions, as seeing the last guy receive the 'final chop' argues against taking over the job.*

The ambulance was starting to leave as Sloan and Adam reached the gathered Army pilots. Having watched the Russian pilot make the journey from the fallen P-40 pilot back to the Army flight line, Adam sincerely hoped no one needed a ride to the aid station. Getting shot or a bone broken was bad enough. Having the resultant wounds shaken because some idiot didn't understand the concept of suspension versus terrain just made things far worse.

Sloan and Adam were met with sullen looks from the Army pilots as they approached. Noting the hard looks on the men's faces, Adam began to wonder if Sloan was the brightest person in the world. It didn't take a particularly difficult math equation to figure out there were a whole lot more *Wildcats* than P-40 / P-39s sitting on the other end of the runway.

Sure that's because their boss is an idiot, but that's probably not what is going through their mind right now, Adam thought. No, right now they're just wondering if we're yellow.

Slowing slightly and stepping to Sloan's side, Adam started scanning over the gathering men figuring out who was the most likely to start trouble. Half of stopping a really bad fight was annihilating the biggest bastard out of the group—it tended to make the rest of the pack hesitate or get pissed off. Given that the Army pilots already looked in the mood to lynch someone, Adam didn't think it'd be possible to get them more pissed.

"Any word on Colonel Perry?" Sloan asked as the ambulance pulled up. The Army pilots looked at one another, then towards a slightly older captain standing near the center of their group.

"He's dead," the man replied.

"That's 'he's dead, Sir,'" Adam snapped. Sloan held up his hand as the captain bristled.

Yes, I called your boss an idiot to his face, Adam glared back at the man. *So I'm a hypocrite, but I am a correct one.*

Before they could say anything else the Russian ambulance slipped into reverse and began coming back towards the gathered group. Stopping a few feet away with a rock on the brakes and several screams, the vehicle's driver threw open the door. To Adam's shock, a petite brunette in a light brown, skirted uniform swung her legs out with a flurry of curses. The woman's face was thin and drawn, and she looked as if she was not far past her sixteenth birthday despite her body language as she strode over to the gathered group.

"Who here is in charge?" she asked in heavily accented English, as the ambulance's rear doors opened to reveal two orderlies.

"I am," Lieutenant Colonel Sloan said without hesitation or a glance at any of the Army pilots present. Seeing motion out of the corner of his eye, Adam saw that the Marine squadrons' remaining flight leaders had made their way down the tarmac. With a start he realized that both Cobb brothers were missing.

Oh damn, Mrs. Cobb, you're about to have some bad news, Adam thought. Then he turned back to matters at hand, as the two matronly orderlies were setting swaddled man down.

"He kept screaming for us to stop, he had to render his report," the driver snapped, clearly agitated. "It is quite ridiculous." The smell of burnt flesh was overpowering as the wind changed direction, and several men began to step away with muffled curses.

The only reason Adam recognized Major Price on the gurney was the man's uniform. His head swathed in a seeping bandage that covered his entire crown and the right side of his rugged features and heavily bandaged left arm in a sling, Price had obviously had a bad day.

"Sweet Jesus," Sloan said in shock.

"Sir…" Price murmured. "Sir!" he said, the sound almost a scream.

"Major Price, I'm here!" Sloan said, realizing the man was in shock. Price turned and looked at the Marine Lieutenant Colonel.

"Sir, we have engaged and destroyed enemy bombers…" Price gasped from the stretcher, trying to set up.

"Understood, Major Price," Sloan said gently. "I'll ask you more later—you are dismissed."

"Yes…yes, Sir," Price said, starting to sag. The orderlies quickly bundled him and lifted him back into the ambulance. The driver, shaking her head, hopped back into the ambulance's cab and took off straight down the runway.

Don't blame her, Adam thought. *I think everyone who is coming back has made it in.*

Sloan turned and watched the ambulance go. Adam, reading his body language, could tell that the lieutenant colonel was quite angry. After a few moments, Sloan turned back around to face all of the gathered pilots.

"Captain Owens," he said, addressing the senior Army captain. Hearing the tone in Sloan's voice, Adam prayed Owens had the common sense not to be surly unless he was ready to fight.

"Yes, Sir?" Owens asked, his voice completely absent of any disrespect.

"You have ninety minutes to figure out two flights. If you don't have two flights, send a runner to let me know and we'll adjust from there. We're going to go looking for another fight," Sloan said.

The Army pilots looked at him in shock, and Adam couldn't blame them. While people could fly two sorties in a day, it tended to wear out man and machine alike.

"Sir, we…" Owens began.

"Captain, some Kraut bastards have roughed up my men. That is unacceptable, and I intend to communicate that to them in no uncertain terms. We're here to kill Germans, and it's time that we got to work."

Damn, didn't take him long to come around, Adam thought with great pride.

Morton Ranch
1700 Local
23 December 1965

"My God," Jo said quietly. "You really hated them, didn't you?" She was looking at Adam in quiet shock, her face pale as he finished his recounting.

"With all my heart," Adam said, his voice cold as he stared at the map. "I hate everything those Nazi bastards represented. Still do, especially now with everything else that has come to light after the German Revolution," Adam said.

"But the new German government immediately closed all the camps and…" Tabitha began.

"Is it any good renouncing murder after you've strangled your first victim? Your hundredth? Or does it take twenty million for it to become a fuc…freakin' statistic?" Adam asked, his face a mask of restrained fury. Taking a deep breath, he pushed back from the table.

"Dad, where are you going?" Jeff asked, suddenly concerned.

"I need to take a walk," Adam said, then put his hand out as Jo started to get up. "Alone please." With that, he walked quickly out the front door, shutting it hard enough to be just short of a slam.

Jeff looked over at Sam Cobb. The former Marine was obviously reflecting on something himself, thoughts that did not give him great pleasure.

"Uncle Sam, Mr. Haynes said that you were missing when he had landed," Tabitha said, obviously desperate to change the topic. "Where were you?"

"He was meeting the love of his life," Nat said grimly. Sam whipped his head around to look at her.

"Present company excluded," he replied. Nat gave him a wan smile and patted his hand.

"I am not jealous of the dead," Nat said to him softly. "We Russians are familiar with loss, Samuel."

"Still, love of my life would be a bit much," Sam replied.

"I am not saying you still yearn for her," Natalia chided with a gentle, sincere smile. "I am only saying that she has a room in your heart that I will never be able to enter. But that is another story for some other time, Tabitha."

Tabitha's tape recorder popped to a stop.

"Yeah, that it definitely is," Tabitha said quietly. "As I am out of tape."

"Well then," Jeff said. "Uh, Mr. Cobb, is Dad going to be…"

"He'll be fine son," Sam said, standing up. "Why don't you two kids stay in here and figure out how Tabitha's going to type all of this up while we old folks go make supper?"

Jeff was smart enough to recognize a dismissal when he heard one.

"Will do," Jeff replied, looking over at Tabitha.

Jeff watched as the older adults all shuffled out of the dining room, closing the door behind them.

"Your Dad flew just a teensy bit off the handle there, didn't he?" Tabitha asked, her face changing to a scowl as if by magic. "Is he always that much of an asshole?

Well I guess we can get that first fight out of the way before we start dating, Jeff mused, his lips pursed.

"Some people don't take kindly to prying," he responded levelly.

Tabitha gave him a withering look as she moved around the table gathering her materials.

"You don't get it, do you?" she asked. "You ever wonder why I'm a historian?"

Jeff's face remained expressionless.

"No, but do tell," he said, wincing inwardly at how sneering his tone was.

Tabitha slammed down the book in her hand.

"Because, you idiot, some of us want to know why we don't have a father," she seethed. "Why our aunt is a damn spinster who's never even so much as looked at another man in over twenty years. And, finally, just what makes people think killing one another is the damn answer to the world's problems!"

Jeff could hear the pain in Tabitha's words and started to get up to go to her.

"No," Tabitha said, holding her hand up. "Don't even start to come over here and comfort me…"

Jeff ignored her, stepping close even as she started to shove at him. Once more he was amazed at her strength, the push stronger than some he'd received on the playing field.

Fighting through it, he suddenly started as he felt her leg coming off the ground, then stopping.

I think I just nearly got kneed in the nuts, he thought to himself. Sobbing quietly so as not to bring the adults running, Tabitha slumped against him, giving up and letting him hold her as she cried.

"I'm sorry," Jeff said.

"Not as sorry as you almost were," she said, then laughed. She wrapped her arms around him, taking a deep breath.

"You don't understand, Jeff," she sighed. "I keep trying to make sense of it all…and I can't. How do people convince themselves the best way of solving their problems is to send their young men off to kill one another?"

"Because some people believe that there are things more important than their own lives," Jeff replied. "Things like freedom…"

"Freedom's just a word, Jeff. I'd rather have my father than a damn word," Tabitha replied.

"I don't think he'd say the same," Jeff replied.

"I know, and sometimes I hate him for it," Tabitha replied. She gave Jeff one last squeeze then stepped back a bit.

"You know, my mother never mentioned Adam had a son," Tabitha said.

"That's because your mom probably thinks I don't like her," Jeff replied. Tabitha looked at him in shock.

"You don't like my mother?!" she asked indignantly.

"Hey, you're the one who just called my dad an asshole," Jeff replied, shrugging. Tabitha's eyes narrowed.

"And just what don't you like about my mother?" she asked.

"Hey, I said she *thinks* I don't like her," Jeff responded with a smile.

"So you're saying that you do like her?" Tabitha queried.

"Why, are you asking?" Jeff teased.

"It's not polite to answer a question with a question," Tabitha snapped.

"It's not polite to think about kneeing a man you just met in the balls," Jeff replied. "Sure didn't slow you down.""

"Has anyone ever told you that you are very, very aggravating?" Tabitha asked, cocking an eyebrow.

"Only your mother," Jeff replied with a smile. To his surprise, Tabitha put her arms behind his neck and drew him in for a kiss.

"You know, this could get kind of awkward if things work out with your Dad and my Mom," she said quietly after they had broken off.

Oh shit, Jeff thought, the scent of Tabitha's vanilla lotion beguiling him.

"This could get awkward if your grandfather walks in," Jeff replied, leaning in to kiss her again. This time he felt her lips part, and he took full advantage of the invitation.

"Yet you just French kissed me," Tabitha gasped when they broke again. "And I get the feeling this isn't the first time you've kissed someone."

"Funny, I didn't notice you having trouble keeping up with me," Jeff said gently, rubbing her back as he tried to lean his hips away from hers.

"Is that a problem?" Tabitha asked, pulling him back towards her.

"No, not really," he said. "But we really better stop, or this could be embarrassing."

Tabitha gave Jeff a knowing smile as she let him go.

"I guess we better finish clearing off the table," she replied. "But I do want to finish...*talking* later."

"After dinner?" Jeff asked.

"Sounds like a plan. Speaking of which," Tabitha sniffed, the smell of cooking meat wafting into the dining room, "I think Granddad is making pepper steak."

Jo found Adam in their cabin, sitting on the bed with a photograph frame in his hands. She knew the two pictures in it without even looking, thinking back to Nat's words.

If it's true the dead wall off rooms in someone's heart, I have to wonder if his heart has a no vacancy sign right now, she thought, a slight tremor of fear going through her. Well, I'm a big girl, and it's not like I don't have my own deaths to deal with.

With grim determination, she stepped into Adam's room.

"Jeff and Tabitha seem to be hitting it off quite well," she said quietly. Adam looked up at her, and she saw that his eyes were glistening.

"Might want to warn your daughter off," Adam started. "That boy's family doesn't have the best luck in relationships."

"I think Tabitha can take care of herself," Jo said, then gave a slight smile. "Besides, it's not like her family tree doesn't have some pruned branches either."

There was a moment's silence as Jo got on the bed. After a moment, Adam wrapped his arms around her.

"I guess, in retrospect, that you're a teacher, not a nurse—that might be all it takes," he said.

"You've never told me about your first fiancée," Jo said quietly.

Adam looked at her quizzically.

"I figured it was ancient history, not to mention impolite."

"Adam, you still have her picture," Jo said. "As a wise Russian just recently said, 'I am not jealous of the dead.'"

Adam grimaced. Jo looked down as the worn, torn picture of his first fiancée. It was hard to tell what the woman looked like due to the fold lines, smudges, and what looked suspiciously like a blood stain on the picture. Still, from what Jo could see in the faded black and white image, the woman had an oval face and dark, loving eyes.

"Zepherine was her name," Adam said. "She was…"

They were interrupted by a shriek from the direction of the main house. Jo stood up in alarm.

"That was Tabitha!" she said, dashing with a mother's speed to the front door of the guest house. Adam was a half step behind her initially, but was the first to the door. Opening it, he sprang through it to see his son running towards him.

What in the hell? Adam thought, right up until he saw a snow covered Tabitha come around the house's corner. Cutting like he was dodging a linebacker, Jeff zigged just in time to dodge a well-formed snowball that should have hit him in the head. Adam, displaying that he hadn't lost many of his own reflexes, ducked to the side.

Unfortunately, that left Jo, worried for her daughter, standing right in the missile's path. There was a moment of stunned silence as Tabitha, Jeff, and Adam all regarded Jo as the older woman slowly wiped cold snow off her face. Fixing her daughter with a glare, Jo bent down to begin making her own weapon.

"Um, Dad, dinner's ready," Jeff said, edging away from Jo.

"You know, when I first taught you to make a snowball, I never thought I'd be a victim of my own teaching," Jo said evenly. "I'm glad to see that you listened to at least one thing I told you."

Calm Jo is not a good Jo, Adam thought, feeling slight sympathy for Tabitha.

"Mom, I'm sorry," Tabitha said, backing up.

"Oh, you've done nothing wrong, my dear daughter," Jo said. Pivoting on one foot, she suddenly turned and pelted Adam directly in his face.

"Nothing, that is, except hit the wrong person," Jo said triumphantly, then started running towards the house.

Afterword

If you like this story, please rate it on Amazon and Goodreads. Then, after you rate it, please tell your friends. Constructive criticism is also welcome.

Everyone has their favorite aircraft. While my all-time favorite is the P-47, I've always been partial to the *Wildcat*. Often outnumbered and outclassed, the *Wildcat* was seldom outfought thanks to the skill and bravery of those John B. Lundstrom dubbed "The First Team." Even though the tough Grumman saw only limited use in the European Theater of Operations, throughout this short story I've relied on Eric M. Brown's *Duels in the Sky* for assessing the FM-2/F4F's chances versus German aircraft. I also suggest Lundstrom's *The First Team* and *The First Team and the Guadalcanal Campaign*.

There is a great deal more to this alternate history universe. Unfortunately, the short story form does not lend itself to discussing the larger pieces of a great global conflict. However, if you liked what you've read so far, read on to get a special excerpt from *Acts of War*, the first full book in *The Usurper's War* series.

ACTS OF WAR
(EXCERPT)

Chapter 1: Careful What You Wish For...

Follow me—You have the advantage of necessity, that last and most powerful of weapons. **Vettius Messius of Volscia**.

Thames River
0900 Local (0400 Eastern)
23 August 1942

London was burning.

Somehow I doubt that this is quite how anyone expected Adolf Hitler's death to turn out, Adam Haynes thought bitterly as he regarded the burning capital's skyline. The wind, thankfully, was blowing away from where he and his girlfriend stood at the bow of the *Accalon*. Adam had the awful feeling that if it had been blowing toward the 40-foot pleasure yacht, there would have been many, many smells he would have preferred to forget filtering their way.

1

PANDORA'S MEMORIES
*Like Guernica, only…*he started to think.

With a roar, a Junkers 52 swept low over the *Accalon*'s deck, its passage so close that the aircraft's slipstream fluttered the white flag hanging from the yacht's antennae mast. An intense, white-hot rage sprung from within him as he watched the canary yellow German transport.

I hope you crash, you bastard, Adam thought, blood rushing into his ears.

"Adam, *my hand*!" A woman's voice broke through his fury.

With a start, Adam realized that he was well on the way to breaking his companion's hand. Although such an act was always unconscionably bad form, it was doubly so when its possessor was the cousin, albeit distant, of England's king.

"God, Clarine, I'm…" Adam started, opening his hand as if suddenly realizing it held a hot brick. His face colored to the roots of his thinning brown hair, making his blue eyes all that more intense. At a shade under six feet, with shoulders broad enough to fit on a man six inches taller, Adam looked very much like a bear wearing an RAF uniform. Unfortunately, when enraged, he had the strength to match.

"That is quite alright," Clarine Windsor replied lightly, doing her best to smile as she worked her hand. A small, wiry woman who stood several inches shorter than Alex in the black flats that came with her Women's Auxiliary Air Force (WAAF) uniform, Clarine was far from weak. Still, her pale face was scrunched up in obvious pain.

Holy shit, I hope I didn't hurt her, Adam thought guiltily. Seeing his worry, Clarine brought up her left hand and brushed back a stray blonde hair, her brown eyes meeting Adam's as she smiled.

"You were just having the same thought I had: wishing you could shoot the bastard," she said simply. "It's understandable, given what has happened these last few days."

Still no reason to try and convert your hand to paste, Adam thought. *You didn't drop the bomb that killed Hitler.*

"Understandable, but most unfortunate," her father, Awarnach Windsor, stated as he joined them at the yacht's bow. "Especially as his escorts would probably blow the *Accalon* out of the water."

Looking up and back toward the vessel's stern, Adam mentally kicked himself for not noticing the eight Me-410s circling roughly four thousand feet above their heads. The gray fighters were hard to see in the haze of smoke roiling off London, but that was no excuse. Smoke had been a fact of life for Fighter Command over the last two weeks, and failing to see an opponent hiding in it was just as fatal as if the assault came from more naturally formed clouds.

"While I am sure you wish you had a *Spitfire* right now," Awarnach observed flatly, "I doubt your efforts would be any more successful than they were previously."

You bastard, Adam thought, fighting to keep his emotions off his face. The tone of Awarnach's voice had far too much "told you so" in it.

"Well father, at least someone was attempting to defend our nation," Clarine observed coolly. "Since many of those who were born to it could not raise themselves from their slumber."

Awarnach turned his baleful gaze from Adam to his daughter.

"Those of us who were 'slumbering', as you put it, merely believed we should have continued to enjoy the peace we had hammered out rather than meddle in affairs on the continent," Awarnach replied. "Instead, that idiot Churchil has now managed to make us forget his idiocy at Gallipoli."

"This is hardly the same as…"

"No?!" Awarnach snapped. He turned and pointed off their port bow, to where London's East End was starting to come into view. "Tell me *that* is not more terrible than some idiotic frontal assault on the Ottomans."

The "*that*" in question was the furious blaze that roared unchecked almost as far as the eye could see. The low rumble of the fire was a constant sound beating upon their senses, but Adam had managed to suppress it by concentrating on the river itself. Now, as if Awarnach had ripped open a shade, the magnitude of Fighter Command's defeat lay before them. It was like looking into a corner of Hell, and Adam was once more glad that the wind was blowing so strongly from their back.

5

PANDORA'S MEMORIES

Once you've smelled burning flesh, you have no desire to enjoy that particular sensation again, Adam thought.

"You can't negotiate with the Germans," Adam said lowly, feeling the rage starting to creep back again.

"Oh? Well then, I am certainly glad that you have pointed this out for me, my American friend. Unfortunately, it would appear that your President and Congress feel very, very differently."

"Father..."

"No, please, I would like to hear this fine young man explain to me why we should not negotiate with the Germans when his countrymen cannot be bothered to even help us," Awarnach raged, his own face starting to color to match Adam's.

"It wasn't our President that chose to accept the armistice with Himmler after Bomber Command killed Hitler," Adam snapped.

"Oh? And what would you have had us do? Were we somehow going to invade France by ourselves? Perhaps build a massive bomber fleet like that idiot Portal wanted to and bomb the Reich's cities into rubble? Would that have satisfied your need for bloodlust? There was nothing more that could be done!"

"Yes, well, *perhaps* the people in that," Adam said, gesturing toward the burning city in front of them, "would have preferred you not giving the Germans over a year to perfect their bombing techniques."

"Perhaps, gentlemen," Clarine said crisply, her hand pointing, "we should be more concerned about that patrol boat's intentions."

Adam followed the point and saw the craft she was speaking of. One of the Royal Navy's MTB-class boats, the vessel was moving away from where it had been standing off the docks and turning toward the *Accalon.* As they watched, the craft began accelerating, signal light blinking furiously.

"Conroy, come about!" Awarnach shouted back towards the wheel house. Adam felt the *Accalon*'s engines stop, the helmsman turning her broadside to the oncoming MTB.

Holy shit, Adam thought, translating the other vessel's Morse code. He was about to say something when Awarnach spoke first.

"My God," Awarnach said, his face paling. "Gas?!"

"Obviously you've never read Douhet," Adam observed dryly.

"Who?" Clarine asked.

"The Italian Trenchard," Adam continued smoothly. "He recommended using gas in addition to incendiaries on enemy population centers. Explains the no-confidence vote a little better, I think."

The patrol boat began slowing, its own helmsman swinging the vessel wide so that he could put it alongside the *Accalon*. Three men crowded the bow and, with a start, Adam realized they were wearing full hoods and rubber gloves. Seeing that no one aboard the *Accalon* was in the bulky protective suits, the man standing in the center reached up and pulled the hooded apparatus off of his head.

Well now, small world, isn't it? Adam thought, feeling a smile cross his face as he regarded Lieutenant Commander Reginald Slade, Royal Navy. Tall, almost gaunt, with a face whose left side was thoroughly scarred from the explosion of a German shell, Slade wore his blonde hair closely cropped.

"You seem to be a fair distance from the North Atlantic, Mr. Haynes," Slade shouted as the patrol boat drew smoothly alongside the *Accalon*, his face breaking in a wry grin that reached his eyes. Reaching up, the RN officer scratched the area around his left eyepatch. The motion drew attention to the damaged side of his face, and Adam heard Awarnach inhale sharply.

"Sorry, I have been wanting to do that for hours," Slade said, ignoring the man's gasp.

"Yeah, I can see how that might be the case," Adam replied with a small smile.

"I do hope you folks aren't planning on going any further down the Thames," Slade continued. "By King's decrees the East End is off limits to anyone not on official business."

"I'm trying to find one of my mate's wife, mother, and child. He's in the hospital or else he'd be down here himself," Adam said.

Slade grimaced at Adam's words.

"Where did he say they were living?" the naval officer asked, his tone brusque.

"His mum's apartment is in Poplar," Adam replied, raising an eyebrow at the other man's coldness.

Adam had seen the look that briefly crossed Slade's face enough times to know what was coming next. The man paused for a moment, obviously choosing his words carefully.

"Unless they were extraordinarily lucky, I wouldn't hold out much hope, I'm afraid. The Germans dropped some sort of gas that got all the way through the area, and then followed it up with incendiaries. Without anyone to put out the fires…"

The officer's trailing off said all that needed to be said. In the last couple of days, Adam had heard a word for the phenomenon that some were calling the Second Great London Fire: Firestorm. The East End had become one huge flame pit, and the *Luftwaffe* had returned for three solid days to help things spread.

"Thanks Commander Slade," Adam spoke after a few moments more of quiet. Sighing at the heavy burden that now lay upon him, he looked up again at the smoke-filled sky, hoping to catch a glimpse of the big Ju-52 again.

"Looking for that arse who came tearing through here about ten minutes ago?" Slade asked.

"Yes, actually," Adam replied ruefully.

"I think that was Himmler arriving to negotiate terms with Lord Halifax."

The disgust in Slade's tone at the latter name almost matched the venom reserved for the first.

"Who knew there was a bigger bastard than Hitler in the Nazi Party?" Adam observed grimly.

"Certainly not that bunch of flyboys who killed him," Slade shot back. "Stupid pilots, always mucking things up."

Clarine chuckled behind Adam. Looking at Slade, Adam was unable to tell if the man was serious or not.

"Heard the poor bombardier blew his brains out yesterday," Adam replied. "Not his fault any of this," he continued, gesturing towards the burning city, "happened."

Slade shrugged.

"No, it's not, but that's what happens when you drop your bombs over a capital city. Sometimes you hit things you don't intend to," Slade retorted bitterly.

Spoken like someone who's never had to jettison something in order to make the fuel equation work out, Adam thought. He'd been a pilot since his seventeenth birthday, and non-flyers' superiority complexes never ceased to amaze him.

"Still. Berlin's a big city," Adam allowed. "No way they could've known they'd drop a bomb that would kill ol' Adolf."

Slade uttered a sound that made his disagreement quite clear on that one.

"Yes, and a 500-lb. bomb makes a big mess. No matter, that bastard is dead now, Himmler took over, and our betters were dumb enough to believe that tripe the Germans were spouting about the *Fuhrer*'s loss making them recognize the error of their ways."

"Excuse me, Lieutenant Commander, but as one of those *betters*," Awarnach snapped, "maybe a better explanation was that we did not want to continue losing men such as yourself in a war that we quite clearly were not in position to win."

Slade turned and looked at Awarnach, the contempt in his gaze almost physically palpable.

"So, in order to save *my* life, you buggered the French, spat on the rest of the Continent, pissed off the Americans, and gave Himmler breathing room," Slade retorted, his voice cold as ice. "During which time he hanged Goering, blew some industrialists' heads out at a meeting, and thus apparently motivated them to build a bloody great lot of planes, bombs, gas, and submarines."

Adam watched as Awarnach's face began to color while Slade continued, obviously taking a great relish in venting his spleen.

"Of course, the bloody Krauts then proceeded to kill a whole lot more of my countrymen. Capital work, your Lordship, just capital, please do not go into anything of importance."

Awarnach's mouth worked in shock. Before he could reply, one of the sailors stuck his head out of the patrol boat's bridge.

"Lieutenant Commander, we have been ordered to a new location," the man called.

Slade continued locking his gaze with Awarnach. It was the older man whose stare broke.

"Would hate to keep you, Lieutenant Commander," Awarnach said, his voice strained. "I'll go back to the bridge and con us out of your path."

"Well, guess we will be about it then," Slade replied, watching the man walk stiffly away.

"So what's going to happen to you next?" Adam asked. "If that is Himmler negotiating the peace treaty."

Slade gave a sideways glance to Clarine.

"I do not share my father's views," Clarine muttered quietly. "Indeed, I think he and the rest of the House of Lords were, and remain, a bunch of fools."

"In that case, understand that this war will not end here," Slade said lowly. "As Churchill said before the no confidence vote, there is an entire Commonwealth that will sustain the candle attempting to hold the darkness at bay."

"You mean you're going to flee to Australia or somewhere?" Adam asked, genuinely curious.

Slade snorted.

"You'd best do the same," he replied. "Rumor has it that Himmler intends to ask for all foreign fighters to be turned over as part of the peace treaty."

"What?!"

"Well, can't have a bunch of Poles, Danes, Norwegians, and Frenchmen hanging around and possibly doing something subversive, can you? Especially not after they killed Milch while there was allegedly an armistice between Great Britain and Germany," Sloan replied grimly.

With a cold feeling in his stomach, Adam could see the government being formed by Lord Halifax agreeing to such madness. Even worse, he knew what the Nazis would likely do with the men.

"I'm flying with a Polish squadron," Adam said quickly, his tone urgent. "How do I get them the hell out of here."

Again Slade gave Clarine a look, then held up his hand before Adam could say something.

"It is not that I mistrust her," Slade said. "However, you of all people know the Nazis as well as I do. Have you heard the stories of how their Gestapo broke several of the Resistance cells in France during the last year?"

Clarine paled, looking almost physically ill.

The thought of being strapped to a metal mattress and electrocuted for hours on end doesn't appeal to most people, Adam thought. *Especially given where those bastards were placing the electrodes.*

"I will go speak with my father," she said simply. "Please hurry—I do not think he would be opposed to making you swim for it."

Taking Adam's hand and squeezing it, Clarine turned and departed.

"Get the whole bloody lot of your men to Portsmouth," Slade said as soon as she was out of earshot. He pulled out a piece of paper and a grease pen from under his rubber top. Scribbling something quickly, he handed it over to Adam.

"You have less than twenty hours," Slade said, meeting Adam's eyes. "After that, you best leave that pretty lass without any idea how to find you and disappear, as I get the distinct feeling that some of my former countrymen will be quite happy to 'help' run down foreign mercenaries."

"Thanks Slade," Adam replied, extending his hand. The Lieutenant Commander took it with both of his.

"No, *thank you*," Slade said, his voice raw with emotion. "You and the others like you tried to save us, even when we have done little to deserve it. Now only you remain."

"I'm sorry we couldn't do more."

"Well, maybe you'll have more opportunity one of these days. Hopefully your President can make people see reason soon, or else it will be too late."

"I think this," Adam said, gesturing towards the burning docks behind Slade, "will help."

"Yes, yes it will. Now get out of here, and see to your men."

With that, Slade drew himself up to attention and saluted. Adam returned the salute, then watched as the man nimbly sprang back to the patrol boat. The small craft backed away under low power, then ponderously turned its bow around. Adam sighed as he heard Clarine's soft footsteps behind him.

"Father is furious," she said softly. "Strangely, I don't give a damn."

"You know that I have to go almost as soon as we get back," Adam said. Turning, he saw Clarine's eyes were moist already.

"Yes, yes I know," she said softly. "And there's no chance father will let me out of his sight until you do so."

Adam could hear the deep tone of bitterness in her voice.

"Life becomes very lonely when you hate your parents," he said chidingly.

"I have half a mind to come with you," Clarine replied fiercely. "That would bloody well serve him right."

"Well, wouldn't be the first scandal an American has caused in this country," he said musingly, rubbing his chin theatrically.

"I am serious, Adam," Clarine retorted.

"I may not even be alive in a fortnight, Clarine," Adam said somberly. "Think about that. Do you really want to throw away your future, inheritance, and family name for some vagabond American mercenary?"

Clarine searched his face.

"Is that really how you think I see you?"

"No, but it's how your father and the rest of your social circle see me. Yes, I come from the right circles and know which fork to start with at dinner, but at the end of the day I am like some exotic animal that is best petted and left alone."

"Adam, *I love you.*"

"And I you," Adam said, fighting the urge to sweep Clarine into his arms. "So much that I will not let you ruin the rest of your life to flee with me."

"What about what I want?" Clarine asked as the *Accalon* came around. "Don't I get to decide the rest of my life, or is that solely the province of my male betters?"

Adam sighed.

Strong women will be the death of me, he thought with a deep sense of melancholy.

"Why don't you tell the truth, Adam?" Clarine continued. "You're scared of what will happen to me if I try to escape with you."

"Yes, the thought of you drowning or freezing to death in the Atlantic does strike me with some trepidation."

Clarine snarled in exasperation.

"Not every event in life ends the worst way possible, Adam!" she breathed lowly through clenched teeth.

Adam turned and looked behind him at the burning London, then back to Clarine.

"Perhaps now is not the time to try and convince me of this. More importantly, Clarine, I have to look after my men."

Clarine opened her mouth to argue, then stopped.

"Then when this boat docks will be the last time we see each other," she replied coolly.

Adam felt as if someone had stomach punched him. He started to reach for Clarine, but she held up her hand to stop him.

"You seem determined to leave Adam," she said. "You are even more determined to make sure I do not leave with you in some misguided attempt to 'save' me. Perhaps it is best then, that I acknowledge you have greater experience in dealing with disastrous circumstances such as these."

The words were delivered with cold precision, and they found their mark with the same brutal finality of a knife thrust.

"I do not want us to end this way, Clarine," Adam bit out, feeling his stomach sinking to his feet.

"If you had stopped after the seventh word of that sentence," Clarine said, her voice quavering, "I might have been inclined to reconsider. Instead, I believe that I am feeling rather nauseous from the smoke and will go below. Have a safe journey, Adam."

With that, Clarine turned and began walking back towards the deckway hatch, moving quickly as she wiped at her face. Adam watched her go, his stomach in knots.

Well, at least it's an improvement from last time I went through this, he thought. Fighting the urge to curse loudly, he slowly rotated back towards the *Accalon*'s bow, and then walked forward to where only the Thames could see his tears.

PANDORA'S MEMORIES

Red Two
North Atlantic
1000 Local (0700 Eastern)
12 September

Lieutenant (j.g.) Eric Cobb, like many aviators, did not lack for confidence. It took a very confident or very stupid man to step into a single-engined aircraft, then take off from a small postage stamp of a warship on a flight over hundreds of miles of featureless ocean. Some people, to include Eric's father, believed that repeatedly doing this was the height of idiocy. Eric, on the other hand, had developed a liking for the hours of solitude, sunlight, and beautiful ocean vistas that were only visible from several thousand feet of altitude.

Unfortunately for Eric, the 12th day of September in the year of our Lord nineteen forty-two had none of the above.

"Okay asshole, I think we're getting a little bit close to the Kraut fleet's estimated position," Eric muttered, his hands white knuckled on his SBD *Dauntless*'s stick and throttle. The "asshole" in question was VB-4's squadron leader, Lieutenant Commander Abe Cobleigh, and the soup that passed for a sky all around them made following Red One's plane a feat of concentration and skill. The conditions were making Eric's forward canopy fog and he had to fight the urge to take his feet off the rudder pedals and brace himself up to look over the top of the forward glass. At several inches over six feet Eric wouldn't have had to stretch far, but taking one's feet off the rudder in the current conditions was not a recipe for longevity. Even though the radial-engine "Slow But Deadly" was as beloved for its handling characteristics as its ruggedness, Eric had no desire to see how well he could pull out from a stupidity-induced spin.

PANDORA'S MEMORIES

"What was that, sir?" Radioman 2nd Class Henry

Rawles asked from the tail gunner position.

"Nothing Rawles, nothing," Eric called back, keeping

his voice level so the young gunner wouldn't think he was

perturbed at him.

Not Rawles's fault our squadron leader is a...

Without warning, the *Dauntless* burst out of the cloud

bank. Eric had just enough time to register the changing

conditions, give a sigh of relief, then start looking around

before all hell broke loose. The anti-aircraft barrage that

burst around the two single-engine dive bombers was heavy

and accurate. With a seeming endless cascade of *crack!*

crack! crack!, heavy caliber shells exploded all around Eric's

bomber, the blasts throwing it around like backhands from a

giant.

Jesus Christ! Eric thought, stomping left on his rudder and pulling back on the stick to get back into the clouds.

"Sir, Lieutenant Commander Cobleigh's been hit!" Rawles shouted.

Before Eric could respond, another shell exploded on the bomber's right side with a deafening roar and flash. Eric felt a sharp sting and burning sensation across the back of his neck as the canopy shattered in a spray of glass, the *Dauntless* heeling over from the explosion. Stunned, Eric instinctively leveled the dive bomber off and found himself back in the cloud bank before he fully recovered his senses.

With full recovery came consciousness of just how screwed he was. First Eric realized that it was only by the grace of God that he hadn't been laid open like a slaughtered animal. His shredded life vest, damaged control stick and throttle, and a very large hole in the cockpit's side were all evidence that several fragments had blasted all around him. Fighting down the urge to vomit, Eric quickly checked both of his wings, noting that the surfaces were thoroughly peppered as he fought to keep the SBD level. Fuel streamed behind the bomber, starting to gradually slow as the self-sealing tanks proved their worth.

Oh we are in trouble now. The two SBDs had been near the limit of their search arc when fired upon. Even with the self-sealing tanks working as advertised, Eric was certain that the damage to the wing tanks had just guaranteed Rawles and he would not be landing back aboard *Ranger*. Swiveling his head, he attempted to find Red One's SBD *Dauntless* dive bomber through the murk.

"Rawles!" Eric called over the intercom.

"Yes, sir?" his gunner responded.

"You see what happened to One?" Eric began, then suddenly remembered Rawles' report. "I mean after he got hit."

"Sir, there was no after Lt. Commander Cobleigh got hit," Rawles replied, his voice breathless. "He just exploded!"

Eric felt the sick feeling return to his stomach. After a moment's temptation to just go ahead and vomit over the side, he fought the puke back down.

"What else did you get a chance to see?" Eric asked.

"It looked like there were at least two battleships, maybe three. Jesus they were close!"

"Okay, you need to get off a position report of those German bastards. Send it in the clear back to *Ranger*, keep repeating it until someone acknowledges, and I will try to figure out if we're going to make it back."

"Aye aye, sir," Rawles replied. A few moments later, Eric heard the Morse code starting to get tapped out. Pulling out his map, he suddenly realized he had no clue which direction he was flying. Looking down at the compass, he felt a sudden sigh of relief when he saw they were heading southwest, away from the Germans and generally towards their own fleet.

"Sir, I've got an acknowledgment from the *Augusta*. She's asking our status," Rawles said.

"Send this in code: Red One destroyed, Two unlikely to return to fleet. Will send crash location," Eric said tersely.

They broke out of the low clouds into an area of open sky, the sun beaming down on the battered *Dauntless*. Eric suddenly felt exposed and began scanning around the horizon. He heard and felt Rawles unlimber his twin .30-caliber machine guns and was glad to see that he wasn't the only one on edge.

Those bastards tried to kill us! he thought, then remembered how close the Germans had come to doing just that.

"Rawles, you all right?"

"I got nicked on my calf, but it's not serious. Are we actually about to crash, sir?" Rawles asked.

"It's about two hundred miles back to the fleet, and we don't have two hundred miles of fuel…"

"Smoke! Smoke to starboard!" Rawles shouted. Eric whipped his head around and saw the smudge that Rawles had sighted low on the horizon.

"Well, you just might have kept us from a day in the raft, Rawles," Eric said happily, grabbing the stick with his left hand. Reaching down the right side of his seat, he opened his binoculars' case and reached in. There was a sharp prick on his gloved finger, and he jerked his hand back. Reaching down more carefully, he realized that while the lid was still present on the case, the container itself was twisted metal.

"Rawles, you still have your binoculars?"

"Roger sir," Rawles came back.

"Let's see what you can see," Eric replied. "Mine are shot to hell."

There was a slight rustling in the backseat as Eric brought the SBD around to begin closing with the smoke. After a few moments, it was clear there was more than one column. About ten minutes later, it was very obvious that the *Dauntless* was closing with an entire group of ships.

29

"Sir, that looks like the Brits!" Rawles said. "I can't tell very well, but that looks like one of their heavy cruisers and a few destroyers heading away from us."

"Great," Eric muttered. "I get to be shot at by both sides today."

"What was that, sir?"

"Nevermind, just talking to myself. Send this location in code also, then get ready to start signaling with a lamp."

"Approaching aircraft, approaching aircraft, these are Royal Navy vessels," a clear, accented voice crackled into Eric's earpieces. "Do not continue to approach or you will be fired upon."

Eric turned the SBD away, banking to show his silhouette and national insignia. The dive bomber initially complied with the movement, then suddenly staggered and began to roll to the left. Eric fought the maneuver, but found that he was only able to hold the aircraft level with the stick pressed almost completely to the right. Looking out at his ailerons, he saw that both were in the down position.

Great, just great, Eric thought.

"Royal Navy vessel, this is a United States Navy aircraft in need of assistance," Eric said once he had control of his aircraft. "Request permission to ditch close aboard."

There was a pause of a sufficient length that Eric felt his arm starting to shake from the effort of maintaining level flight.

"American aircraft, you may ditch close aboard," came the response.

Eric heard Rawles wrestling around in the rear cockpit.

"Sir, I've got the code books in a sack with a box of ammo. Want me to throw it over the side?"

"Great plan, Rawles," Eric gritted. "Get rid of the guns too, don't want you getting brained when we get out."

A moment later, Eric heard the twin machine guns bang down against the fuselage on their way over the side. Shortly after, there was a similar noise as the code books and ammo followed suit the .30-caliber tail guns. Taking a little pressure off the stick, Eric brought the *Dauntless* around in a gradual left-hand turn to see the large cruiser coasting to a stop. The five destroyers accompanying the vessel circled like protective sheep dogs, smoke drifting up from their stacks.

I hope those tin cans don't find anything. Don't feel like adding "got torpedoed" to my list of bad things that have happened today. His right arm began twitching, warning of impending muscle failure, and he quickly grabbed the stick with his left hand for a couple of moments.

"All right Rawles, I've never done this before so I don't know how much time we have," Eric said, fighting to keep his voice calm. "Stand by to ditch."

As Rawles acknowledged his order, Eric had a chance to give the British cruiser a good look. A twin-stacked, three-turreted ship, the RN vessel was painted in three tones of gray, the pattern seemingly random from above. As the dive bomber circled downward from five thousand feet, Eric realized that the captain had placed the vessel athwart the wind, leaving a relatively calm area on her lee. Eric recognized the maneuver as one occasionally conducted by American cruisers in order to recover their seaplanes.

Glad to see things aren't totally different between our navies. The *Dauntless* shuddered, and Eric noted the engine starting to run slightly rougher. Giving a prayer of thanks that Rawles had sighted the vessels, Eric resolved to put the dive bomber down as quickly as possible. Clenching his teeth, his right arm starting to burn with muscle fatigue again, Eric finished the last turn of his gradual spiral down barely one hundred feet over the water and half a mile from the stopped ship. Fighting at the edge of a stall, he pulled the nose up slightly to start killing the SBD's forward momentum.

It was an almost perfect ditching. The dive bomber stalled, the wings losing their last bit of lift barely ten feet above the ocean. There was nothing Eric could do to prevent the nose starting to come down, with the result that the landing was not as smooth as he had hoped. The impact slammed him forward, his restraints failing to prevent his head from snapping against the instrument panel. Seeing stars, Eric slumped backward briefly into his seat and took a moment to gather himself. As he ran his tongue over his teeth to make sure they were all there, Eric felt the airplane lurch and start to settle towards starboard. The swirl of water into the bottom of the cockpit told him that he did not have long to get out of the crippled aircraft.

"Sir, you okay?!" Rawles asked, standing on the port wing by the aircraft. Eric turned and looked at him, the movement sluggish. Rawles didn't wait for an answer, reaching in and starting to help Eric unbuckle.

"Get the…" Eric started, fighting hard to get through the mental fog. "Get the life raft."

No sooner had he said that than water began pouring over the edge of his cockpit. The cold North Atlantic did wonders to clear the cobwebs, and he realized with a start that Rawles was already up to his chest in the water. Kicking his feet free of the rudder pedals and disconnecting his radio cord, Eric pulled off his shredded life vest and started to stand up. The movement didn't come off as planned as the *Dauntless* slid out from under him. In moments, he and Rawles were both swimming in the cold Atlantic, their plane a momentary dark shape underneath them before it slid into the depths.

"Guess we could've left the codebooks after all," Rawles muttered. "Damn sir, you look like someone hit your noggin' with a sledgehammer."

Eric kicked his legs to get out of the water while reaching up with his left arm. He winced as he touched the massive goose egg on this forehead.

That explains why I'm a little out of it, Eric thought, pleasantly surprised he was able to form a semi-coherent thought. *Although it would appear going for a swim in cold as hell water helps clear up getting knocked on the head.*

Worryingly, Eric could feel his arm cramps returning as he treaded water.

I'm not sure how long I'll make it without a life vest, he thought worriedly. The sound of a boat moter carrying across the waves was the sweetest sound he had ever heard. Turning, he saw that the cruiser's boat was almost upon them. Eric attempted to start swimming towards the whaleboat and realized with a start that his legs were going numb.

"Just stay there, gentlemen, we will be with you shortly!" a man in the boat's prow shouted.

Minutes later the Royal Navy lieutenant was proven as good as his word, with blankets being dropped over the Americans' shoulders and rum shoved into their hands. Rawles threw his shot back quickly, only starting to shiver once he got it down. Eric, hardly a drinker, took two swallows to get the rum into his stomach and had to fight against retching.

"My name is *Leftenant* Aldrich, medical office for the His Majesty's Ship *Exeter*," the man began as the whaleboat began returning to the cruiser. Eric saw that the man was tall and thin, his navy blue jacket hanging off him like he was a walking clothes hanger.

He must be older than he looks, Eric thought as he took in the man's youthful freckled face and dark red hair. While his voice was deep and firm, Aldrich looked like he hadn't been shaving for more than a week. After a moment's silence, Eric realized the man was awaiting similar information from him.

"Lieutenant junior grade Eric Cobb," Eric said. "This is my gunner, Rawles. Since you guys actually gave us some warning, I'll assume it's not your fleet that gunned us down."

If Aldrich was non-plussed that Eric didn't give him any more information the man did not show it.

"It would appear that you have met our erstwhile adversaries the *Kriegsmarine*," Aldrich replied. "I take it that you, then, are the aircraft who sent the position report in the clear?"

"That would be us," Eric replied. Aldrich smiled.

"Well thank you for not making my wife a widow," Aldrich said. At Eric's look, Aldrich just smiled.

"I am sure Captain Gordon will explain everything to you if he sees fit. Until then, please enjoy our hospitality. *Leftenant* Cobb, you appear to have taken a pretty good knock on the head. I'll need to check you out once we get aboard."

Eric started to nod, then realized that would be very foolish.

"That would probably be a good idea," he began, then belatedly added, "sir."

Ten minutes later, Eric stood watching Aldrich's finger as the young-looking officer moved his hand back and forth. The two men were standing in *Exeter*'s port dressing

station, a space that was normally the petty officers'
mess. When the heavy cruiser was getting ready to enter
combat, the space was set aside for casualty treatment and
stabilization before the unfortunate subjects were taken to
sick bay below.

"You mentioned something about me saving your
wife from becoming a widow?" Eric asked after a moment.

"Yes, I did," Aldrich replied.

"Sir, I can tell the ship is at Condition Two," Eric
continued. "Obviously you guys are expecting a fight. I got
sort of confused after getting shot up, but weren't the
Germans a bit far away for you to be preparing for combat?"

"Very astute observation, *Leftenant*," another voice
interjected. Eric saw the two ratings in the room jump to
their feet, followed at a more leisurely pace by Rawles. Eric
started to turn his head to see what they were looking at.

"I will not be able to tell if you have a concussion if
you turn your head, *Leftenant* Cobb," Aldrich said, causing
Eric to stop his movement. "Captain Gordon, sir," he said,
nodding towards the door.

"*Leftenant* Aldrich," Captain Gordon replied. "I see
you've been fishing again."

Aldrich smiled as he finished moving his finger back and forth.

"I think this one is a tad bit large to have thrown back, Captain," Aldrich said, stepping back. "We're done here, *Leftenant*."

Eric turned around, well aware of his sorry appearance in a borrowed pair of Royal Navy overalls. Rawles and he had both gladly handed over their waterlogged clothes in exchange for dry clothing, but now he felt vaguely self-conscious in meeting the *Exeter*'s master. Gordon was a man of slightly above average height, with piercing eyes and gray, thinning hair topping an aristocratic face.

"Well, I must agree," Gordon said, giving Eric a pensive look. "I suppose you play what you Americans call football?"

"I did, sir," Eric replied. "For the Naval Academy."

"Barbaric sport," Gordon said. "Can't see why anyone would enjoy watching roughly twenty men bash each other's brains out over some poor pig's hide."

Eric found himself starting to smile as he contemplated a comeback. Gordon continued without giving him a chance to defend American honor.

"But, that's not what you were talking about to *Leftenant* Aldrich, and time is short. Our mission, when you sighted us, was to gain contact with the German fleet so that we could ascertain its position."

Eric nodded, starting to get a glimmer of understanding.

"Since our own aviators believed that the weather was far too much of a dog's breakfast to fly, the task fell upon the Home Fleet's cruisers, or more correctly, what cruisers broke out of Scapa Flow with His Majesty."

"Broke out of Scapa Flow?" Eric asked, confused.

Gordon and Aldrich shared a look.

"You are aware of the armistice signed a fortnight ago, yes?"

"The one between you guys and the Krauts? Yes, sir, I'm aware."

"There was some fine print agreed to by Lord Halifax's negotiators that did not sit well with the King,"

Gordon continued simply. "Namely the part about turning over the occupied nations' governments-in-exile and all of their forces that had fought under our command."

"That part was not covered in our briefings," Eric replied.

Of course, we've been at sea ever since it looked like you guys were about to be knocked out of the war, he didn't add. Eric was certain the term "neutral country" would lose all meaning. if the full details of the USN's actions to facilitate Great Britain's war efforts ever came to light.

Which may explain why the Krauts turned two American aircraft into colanders.

"This breakout wasn't exactly long in the planning, *Leftenant*," Gordon replied with a tight smile. "However, this is of no matter. What is important is that the Home Fleet and a few fast liners did manage to break out. What we did not expect was for the Germans to have anticipated our decision and placed submarines in our path."

Eric fought to keep the astonishment off of his face.

The submarines were part of the reason you guys had to surrender! he thought, incredulous.

"The *Queen Mary*, carrying a large contingent of forces, was torpedoed last night," Gordon continued, either not reading Eric's brief change of expression or choosing to ignore it. "She did not sink, but her speed was greatly slowed. This morning, it was decided to offload her passengers and scuttle the vessel."

Eric looked at Aldrich and then Captain Gordon.

"I am coming to the reason behind *Leftenant* Aldrich's comment," Gordon said with a slight smile. "Before the fleet departed Scapa Flow, there were reports that the German fleet was expected to sortie in order to attempt to intercept the Royal Family and compel their return. They were believed to be another two hundred miles east of the position you radioed."

I am beginning to understand now, Eric thought.

"As I noted, our own pilots did not think the conditions were suitable for flying as dawn broke. Which is why this vessel is currently part of a picket line, and as *Leftenant* Aldrich alluded to, would have likely encountered Jerry much as you did—guns first."

Eric could hear the disdain in Gordon's voice and decided to intercede on behalf of his British counterparts.

"Sir, with all due respect, the weather *is* too bad to be flying," he said bitterly. "Our commander volunteered the most experienced pilots in our squadron, and even then he had to persuade Admiral No…our admiral to allow us to fly."

Gordon's small smile broadened.

"Lieutenant Cobb, I am well aware that you are off of the aircraft carrier *Ranger*, specifically from VB-4. I am also aware that your signal was picked up by the cruiser *Augusta* and that your commander, apparently, perished. Finally, I am aware that Rear Admiral Noyes is under strict orders not to engage in direct combat with the *Kriegsmarine* unless they cross the established neutrality line."

This time the surprise was far too great for Eric to maintain any hint of a poker face.

"Guess I could have passed on tossing the codebooks over the side," Rawles said coolly.

"Unfortunately, *Leftenant*, the manner by which I know all this information also means that your fleet realizes we have plucked you out of the Atlantic. That," Gordon continued, his smile disappearing, "places us in a bit of a quandary."

Gordon turned towards Rawles and the two ratings in the room.

"Gentlemen, if you could excuse us?" he asked, the tone of his voice belying the appearance of his question being a request. Eric was glad to see Rawles follow the two men out into the passageway.

"As I was saying, your presence here places us into a bit of a fix. You, *Leftenant*, are an officer of a neutral nation. More importantly a neutral nation with certain elements who would gladly seize upon your death or serious injury in order to support the agenda of keeping your nation from rendering His Majesty's government any aid. I am sure that you are familiar with the term 'impressment' as it applies to our nations' shared histories?"

Eric nodded, starting to see where Gordon was going.

We fought a minor debacle in 1812 over just that issue as I recall, Eric thought somberly.

"So, in order to avoid any discussions of that sort of thing, I have consulted with my superiors. We can hardly just stuff you in a whaleboat and leave you in the middle of the Atlantic. Therefore, I am here to offer you a choice to transfer to the H.M.S. *Punjabi*. This vessel will then be tasked with escorting the liners out of harm's way, and that is probably the safest thing we can provide at the moment."

Well, no, you could actually return me to American forces or put me on a neutral vessel, Eric thought sharply, but decided some things were best left unvoiced.

"What effect will this have on your force?" he asked instead.

Gordon paused for a few moments, and Eric could see the wheels turning in the British captain's head.

"The effects would not be positive," Gordon finally answered. The man then took a deep sigh, with the breaking of his mental dam almost perceptible.

"The division of destroyers with us is one of two that departed Scapa Flow with their actual assigned crews, full complement of torpedoes, and allotted depth charges," *Exeter*'s captain said, his voice clipped. "The size of the

German force is unknown, but it is highly unlikely that our advantage is so great that we can afford to lose a destroyer before the action begins. The choice, however, is yours *Leftenant* Cobb."

The silence in the compartment after Gordon's explanation seemed to press in on Eric. At least thirty seconds passed, with Gordon growing perceptibly impatient, before the American replied.

"We were briefed before we departed Newport News that our forces were to make every effort to avoid giving the impression that we were aiding RN forces," he said, and watched Captain Gordon's face start to fall. "However, we were also instructed to respond to hostile acts in kind. Those bastards killed my squadron commander and nearly killed me. While I hesitate to give them another chance to finish the job, I'll be damned if I'll make their lives easier."

Gordon exhaled heavily.

"You do realize that when I transmit this news to Admiral Tovey your own forces are going to overhear it, correct?"

Eric shrugged.

"If I end up in Leavenworth it means no one else will be shooting at me," Eric replied grimly. "Seems to me that the situation is bad enough if I force you to take this ship out of the line, the. After what they did to London, I'm not sure I want them to catch the King or his family."

Eric saw several emotions flit across Gordon's face. The man was about to respond when the ship's loudspeaker crackled. Both men turned to look at the speaker mounted at the front of the compartment.

"Captain to the bridge," a calm, measured voice spoke. "I say again, Captain to the bridge."

"Last chance to back out, *Leftenant*," Captain Gordon said, heading for the companionway hatch.

"We'll stay, sir," Eric said, right before a thought struck him. "However, I do have one request."

"What would that be, *Leftenant*?"

"Do you think that His Majesty could consider asking President Roosevelt to give me a pardon? You know, just in case?"

Gordon stopped dead for a second, confusion on his face. Still looking befuddled, he shrugged.

"I'll be sure to pass along your request," the British officer allowed. "Even though I am unsure as to what you are referring to."

Eric smiled.

"I'm sure His Majesty will have someone who can advise him as to what I mean," Eric replied. Gordon shook his head and opened the hatch. There was a quick exchange of words with Aldrich that Eric couldn't quite hear, then the man was gone. A moment later, Lieutenant Aldrich stepped back through the door.

"What is your hat size, *Leftenant*?" Aldrich asked.

"Seven inches even," Eric said.

"I'll see what we can find in the way of a helmet for you."

Eric felt and heard the *Exeter*'s engines begin to accelerate. Aldrich's face clouded as the loudspeaker crackled again. A few moments later, the sound of a bugle call came over the device followed by the same clipped voice as before calling the crew to "Action Stations".

"Well now, it appears that our German friends have been sighted once more," Aldrich said grimly as he walked towards the speaking tube at the back of the compartment. "Either that or Jerry's bloody U-boats are at it again."

Eric suddenly thought about the implications of either of those events and didn't like what he was coming up with. Rawles and the two British seamen reentered the compartment as Aldrich began calling down to the ship's store for a helmet. Eric gave a wry smile as he saw that Rawles had already been given a helmet. The pie plate-shaped headgear looked slightly different than its American counterpart, but close enough that Eric was sure the gunner wouldn't have looked too out of place aboard *Ranger*.

"I see that our hosts have already seen to your comforts, Rawles," Eric teased his gunner.

"I'd be a lot more comfortable with a pair of guns in my hand aboard a *Dauntless*, sir," Rawles said, his voice tight. Eric could see the man was nervous, and he didn't blame him. He was about to make another comment when Aldrich's voice stopped him in his tracks.

"Right, understood, I will send *Leftenant* Cobb to the bridge with the runner while his gunner remains here," the medical officer said into the tube. "Aldrich out."

"Did I just hear what I think I did?" Eric asked, struggling to keep his tone neutral.

"The captain is afraid that one shell will kill you both," Aldrich replied simply. "That would be bad for a great many reasons."

I hate it when people have a point, Eric thought. *At least, I hate it when said point means I'm about to get a front row seat to people shooting guns at me.*

"Well it's hard to argue with that logic," Eric said, looking up as a man arrived in the hatchway with his helmet and flash gear. "Rawles, try to stay out of the rum."

"Aye aye, sir," Rawles replied, his expression still sour.

"Midshipman Radcliffe, you are in charge until I get back," Aldrich said, then turned to Eric. "Given what I've been told, there's enough time to give you a quick tour of the vessel before I drop you off at the bridge. That is, if you'd like a quick tour."

"Certainly, sir," Eric said. "I did a midsummer cruise on the U.S.S. *Salt Lake City*, so it will be interesting to see how differently your side does things."